# THE TALE
## ⤠ of the ⤝
# TENPENNY TONTINE

## THE THIRD ANTY BOISJOLY MYSTERY

# THE TALE of the TENPENNY TONTINE

# CHAPTER ONE

# The Dual Duel Dilemma

"MY CONDOLENCES."

Weak tea, as these sentiments invariably are, but what else is there to say when a fellow clubman announces a death in the family? In this instance, the clubman was Lager Tenpenny and the death was that of his uncle Ratcliffe, until quite recently of Pimlico, SW1. The club in question was the Juniper Gentleman's Club in Mayfair, and Lager and I were comfortably sunk into deep leather armchairs and generous tea-time scotch-and-sodas.

"Did he go suddenly?" Having exhausted the humanitarian angle, I pursued the only avenue remaining between gentlemen and made small-talk of tragedy.

"Oh, I suppose, as these things go," said Lager, studying the rich, red and mahogany Juniper salon through his whisky glass. "Looks as though the bullet penetrated his heart, so I expect he had little time for reflection."

"Bullet?" I exclaimed in very nearly an outside voice and Carnaby, London's finest club steward, raised an eyebrow that was difficult to misinterpret. The Juniper is a topping club with a notoriously hidebound sense of decorum, and it's strongly encouraged that emotional outbursts, if entirely unavoidable, be burst outside. Tea-time at the Juniper is a period of particularly calm contemplation among the snow-capped senior members snoozing and settling deeper into their ways, and indeed Lager and I were the only Junipers present born within hailing distance of the turn of the 20th century. This is where the comparison ends, sadly for Lager, for where I am tall and lithesome and built for speed and cunning, he is designed more along utilitarian lines, like a duffel bag. He has a way of occupying his ground — his leather odeon armchair, to take an example to hand in the moment — as though he's been briefly abandoned by someone looking for a porter.

"Bullet?" I repeated in a more civilised tone. "You don't mean to say he was murdered?"

"Murdered?" said Lager, aghast. "No, of course not, what in blazes gave you that idea? No, it was a duel."

"I still think that counts, in this day and age, old man," I said. "I believe the entire practice has been outlawed for a good century."

"Has it? How meddlesome."

"Well, that's the modern welfare state for you, ruining all manner of innocent diversions. What have the police had to say on the matter?"

"Not much *to* say," said Lager, returning his musings to his whisky. "Other chap bought it too."

"They shot each other?"

"Hmm." Lager nodded. "Rather neatly in the spirit of the whole thing, don't you find?"

"What an extraordinary thing. What was the nature of the dispute?"

"Ah, well, there you have me, I'm afraid." Lager eased out of his slouch and leaned into the theme. "The possibilities are legion. Might very well have been to settle the question of who hated whom the most."

"Who was the party demanding satisfaction?"

"That would be Uncle Ratcliffe's cousin, Hadley. They shared a house off Belgrave Road, the theatre of the most recent hostilities, among many others."

"I thought they hated each other," I said.

"Like cats and dogs," confirmed Lager. "Cats and dogs of diametrically differing religious convictions."

"Then why did they share a house?"

"Part of the inheritance. It all gets rather complicated once you get past the general animosity." Lager drained his glass and put it on the Victorian occasional between us. "It's why I'm here, in point of fact. You couldn't spare an hour or so to have a look-in, could you?"

"A look-in? What sort of look-in?"

"You know, Anty, that thing you do. The old Boisjoly touch." By 'Anty' Lager referred to the diminutive for Anthony, widely employed by friend and, if I had any, foe. And by 'that thing you do' he spoke flatteringly of my modest reputation for untangling the odd ball of societal wool. Finally, with 'Boisjoly', Lager spoke of the family curse, normally pronounced 'boo-juhlay', like the wine region, but in Lager's singular diction sounding more like an Australian speaking French to a child. This peculiarity, along with excellent taste in gentlemen's clubs, was among the few things I shared in common with Lager, whose own last name, Tenpenny, was by popular acclaim pronounced 'Timpinny'.

"It's beginning to occur to me, Lager old man, that you've yet to mention some vital element of this story," I observed. "What is it that you think I might contribute?"

3

"Funny thing about the Tenpenny legacy... ah, splendid." Lager interrupted himself to pass judgement on the timely arrival of two fresh scotch-and-sodas, borne on the capable salver of the above-mentioned Carnaby. "...Uncle Ratcliffe and Cousin Hadley were rival beneficiaries, as it were, and so it's rather crucial, from a probate perspective, to know which of the two men died first."

"Hold up," I said, holding up a demonstrative palm. "Lager, when, exactly, did these two ancestors of yours go off the air?"

Lager regarded me with a sort of baffled disappointment, like a puppy who, instead of an expected treat, receives a hot racing tip. "If I knew that, Anty, I wouldn't be asking you, would I?"

"No, I mean how recently?"

"Ah, well..." Lager looked about him — fruitlessly, I might add, for the Juniper Gentleman's Club has never and will never hang a clock. "What time is it now?"

"Just gone four-thirty."

"Around noon then, I'd say."

"So, if I understand you correctly, Lager, you've left the scene of a crime to come and have cocktails with me," I said. "I admit, I'm flattered, and I share the reflex — when they told me about my father's decidedly one-sided quarrel with an electric tram last year, first order of business was to pop into the Savoy's American bar for a Whisky Sour."

"Good, is it?"

"Let us say that it struck the right tone for the occasion," I said, for this wasn't the moment to debate the use of mechanical cocktail foamers in five-star establishments. I made note of the point for later reference, should conversation wane. "You weren't at all tempted to pay your respects at Scotland Yard, first?"

"Well, I've only just now learned that duelling was against the law, haven't I?" he said, defensively. "Still not sure I buy that, incidentally."

"I feel quite confident of my sources."

"We'll take it as read," said Lager munificently. "Will you come round, then?"

"With taps on my shoes, Lager old man, but I will have to insist that you involve the authorities."

"Oh, we've done that all right. We've got the coroner in. Chap named Babbage. He only lives round the corner, handily enough."

"That's all right then," I said. This set my mind at rest, groundlessly, I was soon to learn. Nevertheless, I settled with my drink back into my armchair. "Doubtless he'll engage with official channels."

Pimlico is a jolly bounce in a London taxi from Mayfair along Piccadilly and through the rarified air of Belgravia, and under Lager's attentive tutelage the driver was able to veer dangerously close to Belgrave Road before skidding down what amounted to a cobbled alley of, on the one side, the private posterior of terraced blocks and, on the other, what appeared to be a brewery and a livery barn. Between them, at an iron gate overgrown with ivy and neglect, Lager bade the driver stop and bade me stump for the fare, in light of his not having had time to visit his bank, what with everything and whatnot.

"I thought it was off Belgrave Road," I reminded Lager.

"T'is, on the other side," claimed Lager. "Well, it would be, if it went through, and if there wasn't another lot in the way. You've never been to the old digs, have you?"

"You know now you mention it, no. I think I've always subconsciously assumed that you lived at the club. Are you saying that you share the battlefield arrangements?"

"No, thankfully, just the posh address." Lager led us between elaborate, wrought-iron newels on stone foundations, demarking the entrance to a leafy residential common formed around a lush, triangular-shaped garden and walled in by three smart, ornate, tall, white manors of Regency period and/or design.

"Welcome to Wedge Hedge Square," continued Lager. "That's me there, at number one, and there…" He indicated the largest, three-story house dominating the hypotenuse of the triangle. "…lies the mystery."

Wedge Hedge Square was, in addition to not being square, unusual in its size. Most such developments in and around the West End are composed of several dozen identical Georgian, Victorian, or Edwardian city seats of the monied class looking onto a shared private garden from which they're separated by quiet thoroughfares. Wedge Hedge Square was wedge-shaped, as was its garden, it was a cul-de-sac, and it was composed of only three fine examples of the sort of thing that got whacked up during the reign of William IV, give or take a decade. They were all of a style, like society siblings, but different and somehow indifferent to each other, like society siblings. They all had gargoyle eaves and tall, bow windows, and triumphal arches with granite keystones beneath hand-carved crowns, fluted columns and black-lacquered doors with silver number plates.

"Who lives in that one?" I asked, with a nod to the remaining address, an impeccably-maintained, recently blanched walk-up with bursts of violets in the window boxes and a rose bush on either side of the steps.

"Number three. That's my second cousin, Victoria," said Lager. "You'll meet her momentarily. It was she who discovered the wreckage."

"What a cosy habitat the Tenpenny genus has established for itself. Must play merry hell with the post, though," I said.

"It does, rather. In addition to every household answering to the name Tenpenny, the addresses are one, three and fifty-seven."

"How quaintly nonsensical," I opined. "Why?"

"Uncle Ratcliffe and Cousin Hadley refused to share an address, so the door is marked with both a 'five' and a 'seven', with predictable results."

We approached number fifty-seven along the edge of the garden. It was overgrown and unkempt in the best tradition of English green spaces, and it smelled comfortingly of rain and heather and earth. A springtime buzz and twitter droned all around and a light wind rustled the new leaves in the old, old elm trees vying for space in the garden.

"I take it, then, that Hadley and Ratcliffe are the remaining threads of two Tenpenny family strands," I said.

"Correct," confirmed Lager. "Uncle Ratcliffe was my late father's first cousin, and Hadley was his third cousin. You'd have to go back some four generations to find two people who liked one another well enough to have children together."

"And Victoria?" I asked.

"Hadley's direct niece," said Lager. "So, my fourth cousin? Genealogy's not really my chief fascination. Suffice it to say that Ratcliffe and Hadley were the remaining elders of two family branches, and now there's just me on the one side and Victoria on the other."

"Does that explain the happy commune?" I asked.

"It does. Wedge Hedge Square is about all that's left of a once-garish family legacy. Some earlier executor divided it in half — number one to my uncle and me, number three to Hadley and Victoria, number fifty-seven, ostensibly, remained neutral ground."

"Then why did the uncles choose to share a home?"

"Spite." Lager said this as though it should have occurred to me, which I suppose it probably should, given what I'd learned thus far. "Neither wanted the other to have the big house to himself. Besides, proximity produced greater scope of opportunity."

"Opportunity?" I asked. "Opportunity for what?"

"Murder." We stopped at the door and Lager produced a key. "This was very much a house divided. Uncle Ratcliffe was of the view that Cousin Hadley had done all that should be expected of him in this life, while Hadley felt strongly that Ratcliffe would contribute best as an *alto-voce* in heaven's choir. They were always experimenting with clever ways to do each other in. The situation might have proved quite perilous if either of them had had an ounce of imagination."

Number fifty-seven Wedge Hedge Square was of that worn, waxy, once-white wilt of grand, fiddly interiors that have been meticulously not lived in for years. It was indefinably reminiscent of some great houses I'd known that had been compelled to close a wing or two as part of a negotiated settlement of punitive death duties.

The bower motif persisted into the main hall, which was itself vaulted and sectioned by extravagant archways, giving the impression of a railway tunnel lit by chandelier. Beneath the arches, from front to back, the floor was tiled in that *trompe l'oeil* tiling that was popular at the turn of the century, in this case a three-dimensional cube pattern formed of black, white, and grey tiles, here and there broken and replaced with poorly-matched understudies.

Large, disused salons and dining halls peeked at us from either side of the hall, hoping we might pop in, even for a moment, but Lager harried me toward the back of the house, where a double door opened onto a conservatory. The external wall was an expansive window of glass and leaded grilles giving onto a raucously leafy garden and bathing the room in natural light. The springtime serenity of the scene was made complete by two elderly gentlemen, lifelessly slumped into their wood and wicker wheelchairs.

As we entered, the room revealed itself to be a sunlit reading room, with bookshelves lining the interior walls, a floor tiled in a chessboard motif, an ornate, iron and ceramic fireplace, and two living people, whom I took to be the coroner and Victoria Tenpenny, in that order. They were easily distinguishable from one another, even prior to introductions. Victoria was of the young, fresh, fast-paced breed of London girls with an art deco bob and fitted waistcoat, the sort of wry squint that would host a monocle if girls wore monocles, and, probably somewhere, a fleet two-seater with an eight-cylinder motor that she's seen from underneath. She seemed the type of girl who could make a fortune breaking hearts if she didn't enjoy it so much that she did it for nothing. The coroner, conversely, looked almost nothing like that at all. He was more in the vein of the London man of affairs — he presented like one of those distracted chaps you see in the City, stalking quickly from bank to barrister and back shouldering great burdens of grim determination and worry about the Bank of England Standard Rate of Interest. Accordingly, he wore a poorly fitted suit that had been made for him between two stone and two stone six ago, and a shock of white hair that had leapt to attention when he'd removed his bowler and had yet to be put at ease.

"Victoria, this is that chap, Anthony Boisjoly." Lager presented me like something he was eager to show the class. "We call him Anty. Anty, Victoria Tenpenny. We call her Vicks."

"No we don't, you insufferable speck," said Vicks, offering me her hand. "Pleasure to make your acquaintance, Mister Boisjoly, now get out."

"Now, Vicks, we agreed," asserted Lager.

"No, we agreed that you should go. You added the bit about coming back with something."

"Anty's ever so clever, aren't you Anty?"

Some questions are dashed difficult to answer, even if you know exactly what the person asking expects to hear. Such questions tend to be of a personal nature, and as often as not concern some quality of one of the persons present. I offer, 'Do you think I've gained weight?' as a popular example, or 'I suppose you think that was funny.'

"Oh, well, one doesn't like to brag." And there you have it. It's impossible to say 'oh, well, one doesn't like to brag' without bragging about, at the very least, one's modesty. "I prefer to think of it as jolly good fortune. Perhaps you heard about the dual, locked-room murders in Fray last year? It was very nearly the undoing of the Canterfell family."

"No." Vicks folded her arms before her and this, somehow, made her taller.

"No? Well, what about the peculiar affair of the ghost of

Christmas morning, up in Hertfordshire? The police very nearly wound up charging my poor maiden aunt with murder."

"Done anything I might have heard of?" asked Vicks, very much in the manner of an auditioning director who's already made up his mind to cast the other chap — the handsome one who doesn't walk like a jackdaw looking for an address.

"Closer to home, you might have become aware of the recent scandal at Lady Selwyn-Bluntly's charity art auction in aid of returning sailors."

"Nope."

"I say you *might* have, had I not stepped in and made a private purchase of the boldly candid self-portrait of Baroness Bellingham. Do you know her? Lovely woman. Not at all the sort of baroness you'd expect to have a tattoo."

Vicks seemed, quite suddenly, fatigued.

"What about it, Doc?" she said, now addressing the coroner.

"Eh? What about what?" The man appeared, as I expect many men do when spoken to by Vicks, defensive.

"Which one of these lethally stupid men died first?"

"How would I know that?" said the coroner. "I'm a coroner, not a spirit medium."

"Mister Babbage, this is Mister Boisjoly," interjected Lager. "Anty, Mister Babbage, corner coroner."

"Boisjoly... Boisjoly..." mused Babbage.

"The one normally suffices."

"Any relation to the late Edmond Boisjoly?"

"My father."

"Frightful mess," lamented the coroner. "Set me back two weeks. Not your fault, I suppose."

"Most forbearing of you, Mister Babbage. These two seem comparatively tidy."

We regarded the orderly scene from either side of two cadavers in seamless symmetry, like one of those perfectly proportional paintings by Perugino, or one dead bloke looking at himself in the mirror. Each had a duelling pistol in his right hand — rather a nice pistol, as it happens, in minutely detailed silver and the same functional design with which gentlemen have been settling disputes for two hundred years. The barrel was short and wide and the devices would have been accurate for very little apart from the purpose to which they had been put earlier that day.

In that regard, however, they appeared to have been a roaring success. Ratcliffe and Hadley were both elderly men in, I would later learn, their seventies, and each had a black and bloody hole roughly where most chaps keep their hearts. The position of the bodies was preserved by comfortable, high-backed wheelchairs. They were handily dressed for their own funerals in black formal wear with ruined white shirt fronts. I took note of a further stain on the lower left bit of the waistcoat of one of the deceased, as though someone had pinched away something they'd found on their fingers. This, unsurprisingly, led me to observe exactly that — the forefinger of the free hand of the body to my left was dobbed with blood.

"And, finally, this is uncle Ratcliffe," said Lager, gesturing to the still life in question, "and this is cousin Hadley. I won't introduce you."

I had a little wander around the installation, hands behind my back, in the style of the connoisseur of the statuary arts. The scene was largely the same from both sides, except for two intriguing differences: a smudge of blood on the floor next to Ratcliffe's left wheel, and next to that a length of shiny, tapered silver. Sure enough his pistol, which was still in his hand and resting on his lap, was missing its ramrod.

"Assuming the men were shot through the heart, as appears to be the case, Mister Babbage," I asked, "how long would you say they subsequently lived?"

"After being shot through the heart?" Babbage said this as though it was somehow immaterial.

"As appears to be the case, yes," I confirmed.

"Not an instant, obviously. What do you expect happens after you're shot through the heart? You slow down a bit? Move to the country? I hope you have no serious plans to enter the medical profession, young man."

"This is the penetrating intellect who's going to sort it all out for us?" Vicks struck a tone of acerbic irony that, until then, I'd only ever heard from truly jaded sixth form Latin masters.

"I expect it'll kick in any moment," Lager assured her. "What's the process, Anty? You take in the ambience, ruminate for a spell, then I suppose the answer just, what? Pops into your head?"

"Something very like that," I claimed. "Just supposing for an instant, though, that there was no way to determine who died first? What would happen then?"

"I think that's a question for Chancy."

"Chancy?"

"Family solicitor," clarified Lager.

"You don't mean Chauncey Proctor the chancy

lawyer?" I asked. Chancy was a chap of our mutual acquaintance who'd recently been blackballed by several of the older members of the Juniper, on account of some long-standing complaint against his father or his father's father or perhaps beyond that. The grievance might go as far back as five generations — the Proctors had been notoriously inept solicitors for as long as there had been ept solicitors against which to compare them. "What's his stake in the affair?"

"It's his family firm that handled all the legalities. We'd have to ask him what happens if it's a draw, but I'm quite confident that it won't be good for any of us — we'd stand to lose the whole thing."

"I don't see how," I said.

"Well, you're not a solicitor, are you?" Lager pointed out. "You see, Uncle Ratcliffe and Cousin Hadley were the last remaining members of the last remaining generation — on the death of one or the other, the legacy is complete, and the entire thing goes to whoever's left alive, even if it's a photo-finish."

"You dazzle me, Lager, with your fleet accounting," I said. "What legacy?"

"He means," said Vicks, imposing herself on the conversation in much the way that a blacksmith imposes himself on a horseshoe, "the vast, unfathomable wealth of the Tenpenny Tontine."

# CHAPTER TWO

# The Base Race
# for Second Place

"You know what a tontine is, don't you Anty?" asked Lager.

"Sort of a common pot, isn't it?" I conjectured. "A shared private fund for whatever it is that people do with money apart from spend it."

"That's roughly how I understand it, too," said Lager. "Except tontines have an expiry date or, as often as not, an expiry generation."

"It's so bewildering for a simple girl to listen to the intricacies of high finance bandied about by savvy insiders." Vicks was drawing yet again on what appeared to be unsoundable depths of sarcasm. "The Tenpenny Tontine was started with equal investments from four cousins — two sets of brothers — in 1825. The objective was to finance various industrial enterprises, such as railway charters, which were all the rage at the time, and trade junkets to Upper Canada. Like all tontines, it was never meant to be cashed out — instead it paid dividends to the original investors and their descendants from the return on the investments. To maintain credibility and stability — and to eliminate the temptation to liquidate the whole thing — the trust was legally registered to dissolve on the death of the second-to-last member of a later generation, selected to be far enough in the future that there'd be no chance that any of the original investors could be alive to care, one way or the other. On dissolution of the trust, the remaining capital, which is by now immense, devolves to the survivor."

"Rather cold-blooded arrangement, isn't it?" I said. "I mean, it seems rather likely that the last remaining survivor would be near the end of his own life when he came into the fortune."

"I think that was rather the point of the stipulation," said Lager. "And probably why Uncle Ratcliffe and Cousin Hadley elected to settle the thing with a duel. The survivor would get to enjoy a bit of time with his money."

"How darkly ironic that they should both die," I observed.

"Sort of a bleak justice to it, I think," said Lager. "But you see the bind it puts us in — if there was no last survivor, the tontine may never dissolve."

"Yes, I think I'm beginning to get a grasp of the gravity of the situation now," I said, but what I meant was that the whole affair was taking on rather a sinister air, and aspects of the scene which initially hadn't struck me at all now seemed ominous. An elaborately decorated wooden display box with silver inlay — doubtless until recently home to two handsome duelling pistols — was open on the mantelpiece. A heavy brass candlestick holder was on the floor. The windows were all closed and locked from the inside.

"Perhaps you'd best tell me about it from the beginning."

"It was Vicks that was first on the scene," said Lager, by way of yielding the floor.

"It was Miss Belsize who was first on the scene," corrected Vicks, distractedly.

"Who is Miss Belsize?"

"The maid," answered Lager.

"Whose maid?"

"Ah, well, she's sort of community property, if you will," said Lager. "No one of us can afford a full-time domestic, so she gives us all equally inadequate service."

"She heard the shots," continued Vicks. "She came here, to the drawing-room, but she couldn't get the door open. She looked through the keyhole and saw the carnage, so she came to get me."

"I see, wait, no I don't — why couldn't she get the door open? Did she not have a key?"

"She did," answered Lager. "We all do, or, rather, all the keys fit all the doors in all three houses. I think it was an economisation on the part of the family construction firm, which at one point had grand plans for the development of greater Pimlico."

"The door was barricaded," said Vicks.

"With that candlestick holder, I take it."

"That's right." Lager shifted one of the doors to display the inside handle, which was now broken. "They'd slipped it through the handles. Simple, but surprisingly effective. Took both Kim and me to get it open."

"Kim?"

"I say, that's right." If one can look about rhetorically,

Lager did so now. "Where's Kim?"

"Kim? Who is Kim?" I asked.

"Vicks' beau," answered Lager, just ahead of Vicks, who had a slightly different subtext to the role of Kim.

"He's just a dim, desperate dollop," she said. "Kimberly Brickstock, for the record, has proposed to me twenty-three times in as many months. I was probably just saved making it an even two dozen by the arrival of Miss Belsize and the welcome news that there'd been a shooting."

"Right, that's me off," said Babbage, who had entertained himself during this exchange by filling out death certificates at a small writing desk. Now he stood and approached the door. "One for each of you," he said, handing grave, ostentatiously drab documents to Lager and Vicks. "The office of the county coroner expresses deepest condolences for your loss. Where's my hat?"

"Is that it, then, Mister Babbage?" I asked. "I rather thought there was a lot more to this coroner lark."

"Tell me, Mister Boisjoly," said Babbage, accepting his hat from Lager and screwing it onto his head, "what is your area of expertise, exactly?"

"Oh, you know, mixology, theatre criticism, the Charleston and, when I'm in my cups, the Shimmy. Sort of a generalist, really, of London ladology."

"You're not a coroner, then."

"No, and I see where you're going with that," I countered, "it's just I recall you organising a formal inquest into my father's sudden eviction from the land of the living."

"Had no choice," said Babbage of a thing which, clearly, still rankled. "Silly blighter shut down the trams in both directions for half a day."

"I know," I reminisced. "I read the letters to the editor of the Times, complaining about the deterioration in service, at my father's funeral. I think it would have amused him."

Babbage blinked for what very nearly became an uncomfortably long time and then said, quite explicitly to Lager and Vicks, "I wish you good day."

"One last thing, Mister Babbage, if you will," I persisted. "When you inform the police of what's happened, might I suggest that you speak directly with a Detective-Inspector Ivor Wittersham of Scotland Yard. Use my name, if you like, he knows and trusts my recommendations with respect to death by violence."

"Why should I want to involve the police?" asked Babbage.

"There you go," declared Lager, as some sort of victory.

"I still feel quite sure that duelling is illegal," I persisted.

"Is it?" said Babbage. He looked at the victims. "You expect this detective-inspector to make an arrest?"

"I wouldn't put it past him, but I merely mean that there are formalities to be observed."

"Yes, I suppose there probably are, now you mention it. Very well, I'll pass it along. Wittersham you say."

"Of the Wittersham Wittershams. Lovely chap. You can't miss him," I said. "Has a moustache that looks like he drew it on in the dark, and dresses like an American visiting London in what he presumes to be monsoon season."

Mister Babbage favoured me with a couple more choice blinks and then was gone.

"You see our dilemma, Anty." Lager handed me Uncle Ratcliffe's death certificate. "Under 'when and where died' he's just written the address and April 6, 1929 — no time of death."

I examined the document. Under 'Cause of death' Mister Babbage had scribbled 'single gunshot wound, emanating from rank stupidity.' I assumed that Cousin Hadley was dispatched with similar severity.

"I do indeed," I said. "Let us piece together what we can. Victoria — may I call you Vicks? No…" Vicks glowered unequivocally, and I continued… "Victoria, you were at home when Miss Belsize came to get you, upon hearing gunshots. Can you say when this was?"

"Couple minutes after twelve," answered Vicks, looking disdainfully at the duelists. "I assume they started shooting at the stroke of noon."

"How very cinematic. And you heard nothing?"

"No. At least I don't think so. Mister Brickstock has the sort of voice that fills the void, if you take my meaning."

"I didn't hear anything either, Anty," added Lager. "And I was at number one, which is exactly as far from the action as number three."

"Then how did you know to come here?" I asked.

"I sent Miss Belsize to fetch him when Kimberly couldn't get the door open."

"Talking of the by now notorious Mister Brickstock," I asked. "What's become of him since?"

"Said he had business in the City." Vicks spoke the words 'said', 'business' and 'City' as though they might easily have stood in for 'claimed', 'friends' and 'the Vatican'. "I've little doubt he'll be back shortly."

"And the mysterious Miss Belsize?"

"Probably packing the silverware, now the coast is clear," suggested Vicks.

"Ha!" blurted Lager. "She's joking."

"Is that the bell pull?" I took note of an embroidered band next to the fireplace.

Lager and Vicks shared a glance.

"Miss Belsize doesn't like us to use it," said Lager.

"I'm sure she doesn't care one way or the other," opined Vicks. "But she won't answer."

"I think we can all agree that these are exceptional circumstances." I pulled the silk belt and found it unyielding. I put my back into the second time, and the bell pull cranked rustily and uneasily downward, and then slowly withdrew, and as it did a soft chaos of jingles came to us over the still air, as though from all directions.

"Fancy that," said Lager. "It works."

Moments later the screech of the front door followed the bells, and we all looked down the hall. A stout, firm woman in a patchwork maid's uniform entered with a bucket and mop, and stamped determinedly toward us.

"You lot still here?" said, presumably, Miss Belsize, as she entered the reading room. She was a middle-aged maid with a hard complexion and pewter-wire hair making a mass escape from a sloppy bun.

"Ah, Miss Belsize." Lager spoke with a sudden and unexpected authority, and then lost his nerve. "It was Mister Boisjoly here that rang."

"Was that you making all that racket?" said the maid with a distinctly prosecutorial tone. I felt certain that she already knew that it was indeed I who was making all that racket.

"Where have you been anyway?" asked Vicks.

"I was at number three, weren't I?" Miss Belsize planted her mop in her bucket like a flag on unclaimed land.

"What were you doing at number three?" pursued Vicks.

"Never you mind what I was doing at number three."

"Miss Belsize, it's my house."

"Oh, very well, if you're going to make a fuss," conceded the maid. "I went to take in the laundry." Miss Belsize issued me a conspiratorial wink, as though recruiting an ally. "Thought it might rain, you see."

"*I* took in the laundry," countered Vicks.

"Least you could do. Anyway, I had a bit of a well-earned lie-down." Again Miss Belsize appeared to confide to me an aside: "Had a trying day, you know."

"So I understand," I sympathised. "Perhaps you'd like to tell us about it."

Miss Belsize steadied herself against her mop, like a seasoned first mate leaning against a mast, preliminary to recounting a rollicking seafaring yarn. "Lucifer pulled down the bedding."

"That sounds very trying."

"T'was," she confirmed. "Had to re-do the piller cases."

"Sounds like you had a narrow escape, Miss Belsize," I sympathised. "When would you say it was, roughly, that the Prince of Darkness interfered with your washing?"

"She means Satan the Scots Terrier," elucidated Lager. "Wire-haired havoc on four legs. Of highly disreputable parentage and origins which are the subject of much conjecture. Uncle Ratcliffe was of the view that Cousin Hadley had the animal specially-bred in a weapons laboratory in the service of the nation's enemies."

"And this spirited animal pulled the linen from the clothesline at, one would hazard, quarter of twelve?" I speculated for the benefit of Miss Belsize.

"Just so."

"Drawing you into the yard of number three, from where you were able to hear the exchange of two shots at high noon."

"That's right." Miss Belsize made an unconvincing pistol of her forefinger and thumb and aimed it, first, at Uncle Ratcliffe. "Bang," she said, before turning her deadly aim on Cousin Hadley. "Then, not two seconds later, bang again."

"Which caused you to hasten to the reading room and endeavour to gain entrance…"

"How's that now?" asked Miss Belsize.

"You rushed here, to this room, and found the door locked," I clarified.

"I didn't rush nowhere," she clarified right back. "Not with my gout."

"But you heard gunfire?" I asked.

"I've just said so."

"And you came here."

"Sure," said the maid, as though making a point that should have been obvious. "It was lunch time."

"You didn't come running in response to the sound of gunshots."

"Got enough of my own business to mind, don't I."

"A most tactful domestic policy, Miss Belsize," I said. "But what was it then, that inspired you to try that door?"

"Why should I take my meals below stairs when there's all this room and a nice view of the garden?"

"You normally dine here in the reading room?" I asked.

"It was regarded as neutral territory by the opposing camps," explained Lager. "Uncle Ratcliffe occupied the first floor and Cousin Hadley the second. The ground floor was, by agreement of mutual animosity, reserved for visitors, the bearding bank and/or government officials, and shouting matches."

"A very civilised arrangement," I declared. "It's not every family that can afford the luxury of its own Belgium. You tried your key, I take it, Miss Belsize."

"I did." The maid nodded and produced from her apron a modest collection of barrel keys on an iron ring. "Still couldn't open the doors, though. So I looked through the keyhole and saw them two, just like you see them now."

"So you called upon Miss Tenpenny at number three."

"I did. She come with that fat bloke, and they couldn't open the door neither, so Miss Victoria sent me to fetch Mister Tristian." By whom, I just then recalled, Miss Belsize meant Lager, whose real name was, of course, not actually Lager. As for the fat bloke, I had already deduced that she was making reference to Kimberly Brickstock.

"Then you and Mister Brickstock were able to force the door, is that right Lager?" I asked.

"Just so." He seemed to draw something reassuring from the question.

"And this is just how you found everything?"

"Exactly, Anty." Lager cast Vicks a triumphant glance. "We haven't touched a thing."

I paced from the door to the windows, which I

24

examined carefully, and then back to the doors, which I also evaluated as one, if it's not being immodest, with a greater than average experience of locked doors. Then I circumnavigated the room, stopping before the fireplace to turn and face the assembly.

"Well, Anty?" said Lager, his voice a schoolboy quiver of hope and naive credulity. "Have you got it sorted?"

"Not as such, Lager, no, I don't," I confessed. "But we're going to have to preserve the scene until the arrival of Scotland Yard, when I'll be able to elucidate further."

"Oh, stellar work, Tristian," said Vicks with the subtlest hint of insincerity. "Your mate's really simplified things."

"What is it, Anty? Why is it so terribly urgent that the police be involved?"

"Because, Lager old bean," I said, "though by all appearances this room was securely locked from the inside, there can be no doubt that one or both of these men was murdered by someone else."

# CHAPTER THREE

# The Hairier Terrier Barrier

"This Wittersham chap, you'd say he was sound, would you, Anty?"

Lager and I had retired to the front door landing of number fifty-seven to await the arrival of the inspector. Miss Belsize and Vicks had been swept away on a wave of ambivalence and returned to whatever it is they'd been doing prior to the discovery of a locked room murder in their midst, as women so often will.

"Oh, perhaps a bit procrustean in his approach to crime-solving," I mused, "but taken as a whole one of the better breed of apple. It was he who worked so gamely to hang my old coxswain Fiddles Canterfell for the murder of his uncle and grandfather."

"You seem to be rather taking the charitable view."

"I'm nothing if not a sportsman," I said. "In any case, we spent Christmas together, when he tried to fit my Aunty Azalea up for the brutal murder of a war hero. Sort of thing that brings chaps together, don't you know."

"Respects your view then, does he?"

"I'm among his most trusted advisors," I assured him. "It's been months since he last threatened to have me arrested."

"That's all right then." Lager lit a cigarette and appeared to brood on the triangular square. "I don't mind saying, Anty, that I wouldn't object a bit if it was discovered that my poor uncle had outlived cousin Hadley by a crucial couple of seconds. I mean, it's all a dreadful tragedy and all that, but there's a tremendous amount of lolly locked up in that tontine, and it's not as though Vicks has need of it."

"Does she not?" I asked. "I would have thought that you and she were about on equal footing, speaking strictly spondoolickly."

"On paper, I suppose, we are." Lager drew on his cigarette and then regarded it with a vague air of disappointment, as though he felt that it was failing to provide value for money. "Unless that paper includes the society pages, where she wields a decided advantage in the form of a keen suitor who also happens to be the scion of one of the City's richest brokerage houses."

"The constant Mister Brickstock," I surmised.

"The very one," confirmed Lager. "Poor blighter's potty for the girl. She keeps putting him off, as your modern girl will, don't you know, but it's just forestalling the inevitable."

"You expect her to succumb one day to his many charms?"

"Stands to reason, doesn't it?"

"Does it?" I asked. "Please explain. Don't hesitate to employ diagrams."

"Well, I've just said, haven't I? The man practically reeks of the root of all evil, the jammy plonk."

"Has he nothing else to recommend him?"

"He's all right. Has a rather irksome way of acting as though the accumulated fortune of five generations of stout-hearted market-makers is a product of his own native cunning, when we all know the only business he ever has in the City is popping round to kid his uncles into raising his allowance, but that aside he's a round enough egg. And as I say, he's lousy with the lucre." Lager found in this a generous vein of fresh slander, and continued to mine it, "That ought to be enough for any girl."

"That's your fashionable flapper for you, Lager old bean," I lamented. "They will insist on two-sided conversation over the breakfast table and the occasional kind word. Really, there's no satisfying girls, these days."

"You know, Anty…" Lager met my pop-eyed gaze with a sceptical squint,"…I never quite know when you're being serious."

"You'd be surprised how often I hear that."

A spirited clatter and grumble drew our attention to the door of number three and the return to the field of play of Miss Belsize, bearing a heavy cauldron. She tacked unsteadily across the square toward number one and as she did a couple of young potatoes and a half a carrot made good their escape from the pot.

"Her speciality," explained Lager. "Irish stew. I'm not sure how it's technically distinguished from her two other staples — mutton stew and something she calls 'jumble' — and I've never dared ask, but it's one or the other for dinner tonight, if you're staying."

"I take it that Miss Belsize does the cooking for all three houses and then does the rounds."

"All four houses, if you count numbers five and seven,

28

and she does."

"You're very fortunate to have found her," I claimed, as we watched the maid spill a portion of Irish mutton jumble onto the outer landing of Lager's house. "That sort of dedication to domestic duty isn't easily found these days, if it ever was."

"I daresay it isn't," confirmed Lager. "I'm not sure that 'fortunate' is quite the right word, at the risk of sounding pedantic. I think 'up against it' might be closer to the true state of affairs. It was between Miss Belsize and a tavern menial who'd done time for selling cat-meat pies on Cable Street. I'm still not convinced we went with the right choice."

"Does Miss Belsize not give full satisfaction as a cook?"

"Comparatively speaking, I suppose she's all right," conceded Lager, "put up against her talents for burning the ironing and chipping the crockery."

"I assume she's at least affordable."

"In the main," Lager nodded as Miss Belsize disappeared behind the door of number one. "She steals, mind."

"Only to be expected."

"Naturally," agreed Lager. "And in any case she restricts herself mainly to lesser articles from Vicks' wardrobe and the everyday plonk from my wine cellar."

"Jolly decent of her," I observed.

"I just think she doesn't know any better," offhanded Lager. "And she lives below-stairs at number fifty-seven, so if anything of any actual value ever goes missing we know where to find it. Went there to fetch back a jug of madeira that I required for purposes of my own and found an old pair of Vicks' riding boots and what must have been a dozen umbrellas. I think she hocks them."

Lager took a last, covetous draw on the fiddly remains of his cigarette before it burnt his fingers and gained its freedom. He watched the cinders die on the wind and then we both returned our idle attention to the tranquillity and green of the communal garden. A perfumed spring breeze gently teased the uppermost leaves of the elms and I was struck by the cloistered isolation of Wedge Hedge Square, like an undiscovered enclave in London's natty west end. The only houses were those of the Tenpenny caucus, and the only sound was the above-mentioned agitated greenery. In that moment, however, a tremendous cacophony echoed off the walls and came to us from all directions. It sounded uncannily like a mezzo-soprano complaining in time to a metronome.

"That'll be the post," said Lager with a touching enthusiasm for what most adults regard as one of the mundane details of daily life. "I wonder how far he'll get today."

Lager folded his arms before him like a practised aficionado of the turf and focused his attention on the state of play which, following his line of sight, appeared to be at the entrance of Wedge Hedge Square.

"Beelzebub," he explained, "the aforementioned Scotts Terrier, has a positive loathing for all authority figures, a policy which he generously extends to take in sanitation workers, the constabulary, and anyone whom he suspects of having any dealings with His Majesty's Postal Service. He has uncanny instincts."

As Lager spoke the monster was made flesh in the form

of an electric ball of birr and whir, wrapped in a black and brindle scouring cloth. The animal burst from the gates like a sponge-rubber ball fired from a gun. He bounced off the garden fence, ricocheted across the street to the stoop of number one from whence he appeared to shoot straight up in the air before pirouetting into a tight, four-point landing and scampering back into the breach, all the while yapping an urgent and fervent battle cry. Moments later, my old friend and older adversary, Inspector Ivor Wittersham, cautiously craned his head into view. He was instantly recognisable dressed, as he always was, in the unerring uniform of the modern detective-inspector from Scotland Yard; trench coat of top-flight war surplus, broken-pencil moustache, and damp, American-style fedora, brim descending.

The dog seemed to occupy several defensive positions simultaneously, forcing the inspector to sidle along the walk with his umbrella held before him like a sword. As a deterrent, the umbrella had little effect, but the dog entertained himself leaping over it twice before circling in for a nip at the inspector's heels.

As he inched his way along the sidewalk the animal hectored poor Ivor sententiously, as though judging his appearance, scent, manner of dress and, above all, claim to trespass on land very clearly under the jurisdiction of the local Scotts Terrier. Ivor looked toward us with wide, sort of beseeching eyes, like an apprentice bull-fighter who's suddenly found himself promoted to main attraction.

"Is this your animal?" he said, mustering a tone of indignant dignity.

"Lucifer belongs to no man," answered Lager.

"The dog is apparently a general blessing," I explained.

"Like Typhoid."

"I expect he thinks you're the postman," added Lager, then to me, as an aside. "We haven't actually had letter-box delivery for half a year. Usually they push it into a hedge before fleeing, or just chuck it at Diabolus who, as often as not, eats it."

Ivor found refuge on the steps and the dog stood his ground on the sidewalk. It's often difficult to read with any precision the expression on the ungroomed map of your average Scotts Terrier — their exaggerated eyebrows alone give the impression that they are simultaneously and equally surprised and disappointed — but I'd have to say that this one appeared satisfied in a job well done. I had the distinct impression that, rather than frustrating Ivor's intentions to trespass, all this activity had been in aid of seeing the inspector safely across Wedge Hedge Square, keeping to those areas clearly marked for pedestrian traffic. Nevertheless, the dog presented as a committed scrapper — part of his left ear had been amateurishly detached and his tail described two opposing right angles, forming an almost perfect 'Z'.

Lucifer caught my eye with that fraternal esteem with which most fuzzy four-footers and I regard each other, and he spoke a curt "woof", as though to say, 'Right then, keep your eye on that one — doesn't know his footpath from his asphalt.' Then, spotting a butterfly flitting in a disorderly fashion, he scrabbled off.

"What ho, Inspector," I greeted Ivor in the traditional call of the London familiar. "May I introduce Tristian Tenpenny, clubmate, unrepentant wide-bowler, and recently bereaved. You'd know him better as Lager, if you were me."

Ivor climbed the steps and shared perfunctory handshakes with Lager and myself.

"Pleasure to make your acquaintance, Mister Tenpenny." Ivor spoke in a manner seemingly contrived to flaunt his flare for toneless formality. Then he acknowledged me with the warm abandon that has characterised our friendship since its inception, "Mister Boisjoly. Of course you're here."

"Most astute, Inspector," I admitted. "I am. I take it that Mister Babbage, the county coroner, informed you that dark dealings are afoot?"

"He did," confirmed Ivor. "Although he, himself, remains unconvinced."

Lager seized on this, of course, "There you go Anty. Duelling isn't a crime, is it, Inspector?"

"Of course it is."

"Is it?" Lager allowed his incredulity to manifest as a pouty bit of frown. "Are you quite sure?"

"Of course I'm sure," insisted Ivor, then, in stark testimony to his exasperation with Lager, he turned to me for sense. "I take it a duel has been fought on the premises, resulting in one or more fatalities."

"One or more is the precise number of fatalities, Inspector," I said. "But one or more of them are not the result of a duel."

"Don't tell me…"

"I fear I must, or we'll never get anywhere."

"Very well," sighed Ivor, with the forbearance of Sisyphus, facing another uphill climb.

"What we have, Inspector," I announced, "is nothing less than a locked-room murder."

"You keep saying that, Anty…" complained Lager. "What makes you say it was murder?"

For Ivor's benefit, I recounted the key details, "The duel was fought in this very house, ground floor, back. The maid heard the shots and, in time and after preparing a spot of lunch, made her way here, to discover that the room was not only locked but barricaded from the inside."

"So far, that sounds very much to me as though a duel was fought behind locked doors."

"Indeed, but both men were killed with a single shot — to the heart — an eventuality which Mister Babbage assures me invariably results in an instantaneous shuffling off of mortal coils, are we in agreement on that point?"

"Fair enough," conceded Lager. Ivor merely regarded me with the incurious detachment of the practised opera-goer.

"And yet Miss Belsize heard two shots, some time apart," I pointed out. "If both wounds were instantaneously fatal, which of the men fired the second shot?"

CHAPTER FOUR

# More Lore of the Boer War

Not wishing to trouble me further, Ivor insisted on inspecting the scene of the incident alone. He suggested that I had, in fact, done enough already. He's thoughtful that way, is our Inspector Wittersham.

Lager served as guide to the far reaches of the back of the house and I was left alone on the step to ponder the guileless comportment of *Canis caledonia* in the wild as Lucifer went about the thankless task of disposing of the potatoes that Miss Belsize had left in her wake. This put him directly under the judgemental eye of Vicks Tenpenny, who in that moment emerged from the curtain of green that was the gate to Wedge Hedge Square, apparently returning from someplace that dealt in the trade of sticky buns. She held her basket of pastries close to her chest and glowered at the dog, and then shared with him some confidence which, from that distance, appeared to be a cautionary tale addressing the hazards inherent in eating food found in the street. The dog cocked a respectful remaining portion of ear but then, apparently deaf or indifferent to the moral lesson, ate the half-a-carrot.

Exasperated, Vicks undermined her efforts to broaden

Lucifer's horizons by rewarding him with a sticky bun, and the two parted company in cordial disagreement. By then I'd walked the distance between number fifty-seven and Vicks' homebound trajectory.

"You still here?" she asked in a manner that somehow made of the observation both an appalling state of affairs and a matter of no consequence at all.

"I most certainly am," I assured her. "I won't be missed at the Juniper before cocktail hour, and if I'm late Carnaby ices a champagne cocktail like no man of woman born. Thank you for your concern, though. Been shopping?"

"I'm giving tea."

I broke the hard news bluntly, "I've had mine."

"Good job you're not invited then,"

"Yes, lucky break, that. Is Mister Brickstock fond of sticky buns?"

Vicks smiled one of those flat, 'you think you're so clever' smiles that I see so often.

"Mister Brickstock will eat anything that doesn't eat him first," she said. "But these provide me an unassailable pretext to tell him to keep his sticky hands to himself."

"Insidiously clever strategy, Miss Tenpenny," I said. "If you'll allow me, I'll share with you another approach I've heard employed by certain city girls when dealing with unwelcome suitors."

"What's that?"

"Don't invite them to tea. I'm told it's remarkably effective."

"Not really an option, in this case." Vicks said this distractedly, gazing dreamily at the Dog Prince of Darkness as he dug a poorly engineered hole in Lager's front garden.

"I may very well need to keep the oaf on hand as a desperate plan B."

"How fond women are," I mused. "Is that a quote from Browning?"

"Just being pragmatic." Vicks began to wander idly toward her door in that subtle way that people have of moving off and hoping you haven't noticed. "If you do what my dear cousin wants and somehow prove that his uncle Ratcliffe died before my uncle Hadley, then Kimberly Brickstock's going to be the best of very few choices."

"Surely not so very few, Miss Tenpenny."

"Let's see…" Vicks looked skyward and did a quick inventory. "Counting all my suitors with Mister Brickstock's market capitalisation, that makes… one."

"Well off, is he?"

"You don't know the Brickstock family brokerage? It's one of the richest in the City."

"Have they any holdings in hospitality or horse racing?" I asked.

"No, of course not."

"Then I'm unlikely to have heard of them," I confessed. "I maintain a very focused portfolio."

"Well, if you can manage to take my word for it that they're positively dripping in that which makes the world go 'round, you'll understand why I can't put the man off much longer, now that Uncle Hadley's no longer an obstacle."

"*Was* Uncle Hadley an obstacle?" I asked.

"Mister Brickstock probably thought so," said Vicks. "He suspected my uncle didn't like him."

"I see. And why was that?"

"Because my uncle didn't like him," she responded casually. "Used to call him a fat idler. To his face, mind."

"And Mister Brickstock picked up on these subtle signs, did he?"

"He's clever that way."

"I'm pleased to hear it," I said. "The inspector will be keen to have his insights. Yours too, I've little doubt."

"You really brought in Scotland Yard, then."

"I thought it advisable, what with the duel, and the murder, and what-have-you."

"Still convinced it was murder, are you?"

"I am," I assured her. "Can't really say how nor why nor, if it comes to that, *who* was killed, but I feel I've got the where and when aspects of the affair well and truly sorted. It's a process."

"And Scotland Yard doesn't mind you sticking your oar in?"

"The inspector is a strong believer in the creative dialectic," I said. "He gives out as though he resents the intrusion and that he'd have me arrested on the slightest pretext, but it's mainly for form's sake."

"He'll need all the help he can get," speculated Vicks. "I don't know who did it — if anything was done at all — but I know that none of us did."

"A most charitable view," I said. "Is it born entirely of a sweet, child-like faith in human nature?"

"Hardly. It's cold logic — I know I didn't do it. Miss Belsize has no initiative and Tristian has no reason to kill anyone. Not to mention he's too stupid."

"Kind of you to not mention it," I observed. "You don't think that Lager would regard the vast fortune of the

Tenpenny Tontine sufficient motive for murder?"

"Sure," declared Vicks, as she took a step up toward the front door of number three, Wedge Hedge Square, in what would shortly prove to be a dramatic exit. "But he has no claim to the tontine — his uncle wasn't even a Tenpenny."

And Vicks Tenpenny was gone, taking with her, for the moment, a tantalising allusion. This was instantly replaced, however, with a renewed line of enquiry opened up by Cerberus, who yipped officiously and danced about the entrance to the square, heralding the arrival of a stocky chap with a countenance and bearing deftly balanced between bullish and baffled. He was a weighty type, carefully sewn into a three-piece tweed casing by a magician of a tailor, and his deeply dimpled brow was a testament to the smug certitude of the congenitally unsure.

The focus of the inquisition stamped across the road toward me, disregarding the sidewalk in what must have struck Lucifer as deliberate ignorance of clearly stated instructions. The little terrier bounded before the man like a sentient rubber ball and was largely ignored but for one dramatic moment when the bloke stopped, primed his right leg like a seasoned rugby fly-half, and launched a sharp kick at Lucifer's yapping maw.

Of course the dog had occupied five other distinct places in time and space before the kick struck home, and the force of the unmet follow-through spun his assailant 180 degrees, so that when both feet were once again on the ground he was facing back the way he came. He looked about him, established his bearings, turned, and continued his crossing with courageous aplomb.

Finally, he stopped before me and reacted as so many do to my smiling features.

"Who the devil are you?"

"Boisjoly, Anthony, when pleading from the dock at the Old Bailey," I said, offering my hand. "Anty, to everyone else. I take it that you are Mister Brickstock?"

"You've heard of me." He said this with a sort of deliberately casual pride.

"You're the talk of Wedge Hedge Square," I said. "Only moments ago I was hearing tell of the immense threat you pose to the nation's strategic reserve of sticky buns."

"Yes, I saw you talking to Miss Tenpenny." Brickstock spoke with the authority of the local constable confronting a known pickpocket. "You should know, sir, that the lady is spoken for."

"Oh, indeed, she made that very clear," I assured him.

"Did she now." Brickstock made every effort to make this sound as though he expected nothing less. "I'm most gratified to hear it."

"Yes, she left no doubt that she speaks for herself."

"Is that so?"

"With, if it's not going out on a limb," I ventured, "knobs on."

"Then perhaps you'd care to tell me what it was that you were discussing with my fiancée?"

"Oh, this and that. Your name came up. Eventually conversation led, as it almost always does with girls these days, to murder."

"Murder? Who was murdered?" demanded Brickstock.

"Ah, there you take me into deep waters," I confessed. "But you're acquainted with the candidates. I understand that you were on hand today when the messrs Tenpenny ostensibly punched each other's ticket to paradise."

"How is that murder?" asked Brickstock. "Nothing illegal about a duel."

"There is, actually." I differed. "I had no idea that misconception was so widely held. But in fact one or, for that matter, both men were killed by a person or persons unknown, contrary to British common law. There's an inspector from Scotland Yard at number fifty-seven now."

"Scotland Yard?" blurted Brickstock with a strength of emotion that, had we been at the Juniper, would have invited one of Carnaby's more censorious eyebrows. "What idiot got the police involved?"

"Boisjoly, Anthony, when pleading from the dock, etc. You know the rest."

"Can't be helped now, I suppose." Brickstock accepted this gamely, like a tycoon having to knock off another couple hundred thousand pound share offering before he can quit for the day. "Doubtless he'll want my views."

"I expect he's pacing the halls as we speak, muttering your name. Shall I pencil you in for just after tea, Mister Brickstock?"

"Call me Burly," he said.

"Must I?"

"Everybody does."

"Then you must be firm, Brickstock, stand up for yourself and your good name."

"I like it," he claimed.

"That's strangely fortuitous," I said. "Chap at the Juniper — my club, if you don't know it — introduces himself openly as 'Noiseome', a sobriquet levelled on him in prep, because he thinks it means 'boisterous'. None of us have the heart, of course, so we just call him 'Stinker' and let him wonder why."

Burly Brickstock blinked at me in a manner that somehow brought his eyes closer together.

"My club's the Gresham," he said at last.

"Of course it is," I said. "I wish you a most satisfying tea, Barstool, old man. I shall regain number fifty-seven, now — doubtless the inspector is pining for my company."


If Ivor was indeed anxious to see me he hid it behind a brave face. In fact, he hid it behind the closed door of the conservatory, outside which Lager lingered like a lout, smoking a cigarette and flicking his ashes into a ceramic and seashell floor vase.

"Have you left the inspector unattended?" I asked.

"He kicked me out," said Lager, with no hint of grumble. "He's in there measuring things. You quite sure you have all his confidence, Anty?"

"Like a father confessor," I said, "lapsed, albeit, in certain key areas. Why do you ask?"

"It's just he implied that you could meddle for England."

"Did he? What were his exact words?"

*"'That bloke could meddle for England.'"*

"He meant it affectionately," I assured him. "He's said far worse in what I always assume is a spirit of comradery. Nevertheless, let us leave him to his forensics and fossicks, and have a butcher's at the rest of number fifty-seven. I wish to gain insight into the psychology of the recently departed."

"Fair enough. Where would you like to start?"

"The stairs, I believe."

"Back this way, on the left." Lager gestured toward the front of the house.

"Noted," I said. "But I don't refer to actual stairs, in the literal sense. I'm asking about the concept in the abstract — how did two men, ostensibly confined to wheelchairs, negotiate a three-story house?"

"Oh, right — the lift."

"There's a lift?

"There is." Lager sounded as surprised as I was. "Rather an ingenious contraption. Would you care to see it?"

"I can think of nothing else until then."

Lager led us back to the stairwell which occupied a goodish portion of the right side of the house, accessible by a foyer doorway. The steps and balustrades were intricately carved oak and the stair chamber itself, like the rest of the house, was white plaster and mouldings all the way up. The staircase meandered back and forth in two flights per floor, and neatly retrofitted between them was a wrought-iron elevator shaft, just broad enough to accommodate a luxury-model wheelchair.

"Rather a coincidence, both men needing a wheelchair concomitantly enough to cooperate on the installation of a lift," I observed.

"It would have taken a great deal more than that to get them to collaborate on anything," countered Lager. "Nothing short of an act of parliament, faithfully supported by a well-armed division of dragoons. This was put in ten years ago, as part of the switch to electric, along with a boiler to replace the gas fire, put in ten years before that when coal fell out of fashion. Left pipes and caverns behind every wall, like termites. You could push the place over now with a hard look."

"Surprisingly progressive, if I can say that without giving offence," I said. "I had received the impression that the watchword of the latest generation of Tenpennys was 'economy'."

"T'is. You need to see it from a perspective of scale — everything done in Wedge Hedge Square is done in threes. Gas pipes under the street heat and light all three houses and obviate the need for staff to shift coal about the place. Similarly, one industrial electric boiler can provide central warming and tepid water where gas once delivered hissing heat and scalding baths."

During this diatribe on home comforts Lager had led the way into the lift. He selected 'five', from a handsome brass panel with a hand-crank, in case of power outage, presumably, and a row of buttons marked, from top to bottom, 'seven', 'five', 'ground', and 'cellar'. After an impressively steam-era chugging and clunking, we began to rise at a pace approximating that of an overly cautious amateur climbing a sheer cliff-face. I passed the time in idle chit-chat.

"The houses of Wedge Hedge Square have cellars?"

"A cellar," corrected Lager. "There's a single coal cellar underneath the garden, accessible from below stairs of each of the houses. Now it's where the electric boiler makes its minimal contribution to the comfort of the living, and where the service bell wires connect the bell pulls in every room on the square to every servant's hall. That way, no matter where you are in whichever house, you can pull the bell and, no matter which house she's in, Miss Belsize can ignore it."

"Dashed convenient."

"Oh, rather," said Lager, with that upper pitch one employs to telegraph sarcasm. "Particularly around this time of year, when the spring rains flood the basement to the ceiling and put out the lights, the heating, the lift — very handy for the plumbers and electricians who can postpone any big, personal expenditures — a country estate, say, or endowing a chair at Oxford — until they've serviced our boiler."

The first floor — number five — was Uncle Ratcliffe's floor and abode. I never met the old man, myself, but Lager assured me that he was every bit as grim and hidebound as his household suggested. The old boy did himself well, by all appearances — his floor was a wealth of well-appointed sitting rooms and an office and a comfortable bedroom with a high and wide window giving out on the back garden. But there was something fundamentally sterile about it all, as though he'd never quite taken five (floor one), fifty-seven Wedge Hedge Square, Pimlico, to his heart. There were no casually discarded theatre programmes or racing forms or bailiff's notices — none of the sort of thing that makes a house a home. The closest thing to a personal touch was a perfunctory exhibition of daguerreotypes and photographs arranged about the mantlepiece of the salon, a room that functioned as the reception area to the lift. The pictures chronicled the happy childhood of little Ratcliffe Tenpenny, in and about the grounds of one of those baroque manor estates that look incomplete without a peasant uprising.

"This is, I take it, Uncle Ratcliffe, from the days when little boys could be made to wear lederhosen without legal repercussion," I said to Lager. I had surmised as much from the multitude of representations of the same little boy, but it seemed uniquely and eerily egocentric to have so many pictures of oneself as a child. There he was in school uniform, next to what I took to be his mother, owing to the bearing of barely disguised tolerance of the tall, slim, picture of blue-blooded womanhood with whom he posed. Then there he was again, this time in fancy dress as a chimney sweep, accompanied by what was undoubtedly the nanny, judging from her tired and indulgent countenance and exceptional ubiquity among the photographs on the mantle.

"That's the blackguard," nodded Lager. "Deceptively adorable, seen in still life, as are most children, in my experience."

Indeed, the Ratcliffe of some seventy years ago had the sort of face that, it is said, is loved by the camera. Here he is in little top hat and tails, attending his mother on the steps of the manor, and here he is again, playing with lumps of coal under the smiling eye of the nanny. But repressed little lord or irrepressible ragamuffin, pinched cheeks and deep dimples will always tell.

"And this, then, would be your great-aunt," I observed of the tall, patrician pattern of impatience.

"No, of course not," said Lager.

"No?" I asked, cocking a curious eyebrow, as I will in cases when it's called for, such as when there rests some doubt whether or not I'm confused.

"Ah, well, when I say no," Lager followed my eye to a photograph of a marginally older Ratcliffe in graduation cap and gown, standing next to his mother, who was smiling in a manner that looked like it hurt. "I mean, in a specific sense, yes, she's my great-aunt."

"Is this lack of clarity in any way related to Vicks'

cryptic contention that your uncle wasn't really a Tenpenny?"

"Told you that, did she?"

"She did," I said. "Seems an appropriate moment to bring it up."

"Good as any," conceded Lager. "She's wrong, of course, but for the first twenty-odd years of Uncle Ratcliffe's life his name wasn't Tenpenny — it was Coleridge."

"Any relation?"

"Well, no, you see, that's just it — that wasn't his real name either."

"I see," I credibly claimed.

"It's all rather simple, really," contended Lager, though he looked up into his brow in that way people do when they're trying to recall things which are, in fact, not at all rather simple, really. "Uncle Ratcliffe's mother and his father, Terrence Tenpenny, weren't quite legally married, in the strictly technical sense of the term."

"How then, might you characterise their relationship?" I asked.

"I suppose it was in the order of what some might term an illicit affair."

"I see," I said, and this time I meant it. "And what prevented your ancestor from doing the honourable thing?"

"He was rather in the way of already being married — to my great-aunt Beryl, you see, and between them they'd managed to assemble, for lack of a less classist term, a 'legitimate heir' — bloke by the name of Thatcher." Lager focused his energies on his power of recall, now, and aided in this endeavour by pacing the salon. "So Terrence lodged the yet unborn Ratcliffe and his mother, Hespenal Halisham-Lewes, discreetly but luxuriously, at Drab House…" Lager made nodding reference to the photograph of the baroque manor. "When the happy union produced a boy, he was duly christened in the local parish of Gutter Folly with a fictional name — more of a placeholder, as it would turn out — and spent many happy, hidden years receiving the sort of attention and education of which most bastard sons can only dream."

"I think I can see the rest of the story," I said, "as though playing out before us as on a stage — the ageing patriarch begins to feel the weight of the years, the bitter regret for the irretrievable, he summons his absent progeny to him here — let us say this very room, to simplify staging — and, tears in his eyes and atonement in his heart, he folds the boy in his arms and speaks the only two words that matter, 'my son'."

"Hardly," scoffed Lager. "No, Thatcher — the aforementioned legitimate heir — bought it in 1881. One of those African land-skirmishes, you know…"

"The Boer War, I think you mean. It was in all the papers."

"That's it — the Boer War." Lager paused in his travels to award me the point. "Anyway, when Thatcher didn't come home from Transvaal, Great-Uncle Terrence elected to recognise the spare."

"Elevating Ratcliffe from a Coleridge to a Tenpenny."

"Exactly," said Lager. "So, you see, my uncle has an indisputable claim on the tontine. If anyone doesn't, in fact, it's Vicks."

# CHAPTER FIVE

# Seventh Floor for Old Scores, Distant Shores, and Portuguese Man O'Wars

"Are you claiming now that it's your cousin Victoria who's not a Tenpenny?" I asked.

"No, of course she is," said Lager. "But there's every likelihood that she's not Hadley's most direct descendent. Not by a very broad field indeed, if the stories are true."

"I do enjoy a good story," I said.

"Follow me, then, to the wondrous world of Cousin Hadley's House of Curiosities, located one floor above us at number seven, fifty-seven, Wedge Hedge Square." Lager led the way back to the lift and in a moment we were chugging our way upward at the velocity of a donkey tied to a post.

Number seven was as different to number five as any two floors of the same house could be. Where Uncle Ratcliffe's residence was uncluttered whiteness, Cousin Hadley's was a deep-toned chaos of ratan wallpaper, tropical plants in terra-cotta pots, masks, trophies, spears, and swords mounted on walls and panels and plinths, and all manner of crawling, flying, slithering and swimming insect, animal, and icky inbetweens impaled behind countless panes of glass.

"You wanted stories?" said Lager. "This room alone must have a thousand. Wait 'til you see the study."

"Was Cousin Hadley some sort of collector?"

"Some sort, yes," said Lager, studying an enormous hairy spider in a jar of aspic. "He collected experiences, to hear him tell it. *The moments of peril and pluck without which there is no life.*' I'm not sure how much he actually believed the philosophy but he took no end of pleasure in repeating it before Uncle Ratcliffe who was, decidedly, more the retiring kind."

"Not one for adventure, our Uncle Ratcliffe?" I surmised.

"Not unless you count one month out of every two spent in silent retreat at a Carthusian monastery. Do you?"

"I do not."

"Then, no, not one for adventure," confirmed Lager. "Cousin Hadley, on the other hand, faithfully abiding by his empty aphorism, was. His club goes by the aggressively pretentious name of The Swashbucklers Society, if you will. Bloke was always flitting about the world, rarely home. You see this?"

Lager referenced a shelf of little treasures — the jawbone of a venomous snake, a shrunken head, and what-have-you — one of which was a tiny trestle suspending in a place of honour a bulbous dart sort of thing, with colourful feathers and a rather severe-looking stinger.

"Poison dart," explained Lager. "Hadley took it to the

gluteus maximus while exploring the jungles of Papua New Guinea."

"Can't have been tremendously poisonous," I observed.

"There's always a story, with Hadley," explained Lager. "Damned thing stuck itself into his wallet — damaging a picture of Queen Victoria in a most amusing fashion, to hear him tell it — but leaving the sensitive area unaffected. The dart, however, is dipped in the venom of the Hooded Pitohi, a highly toxic nesting bird, if you will. The upshot was that the tribesmen took Hadley to be some sort of Greek hero, or whatever the equivalent is in Papua New Guinea Classical Mythology, and invited him back to base for a slap-up rite of tribal membership followed by a night of... I'll speak euphemistically and spare your young ears... 'hospitality' from the chief's daughters."

"Daughters?"

"Plural, yes," confirmed Lager. "You're getting the picture, I take it. No telling how many little Hadleys there are running about the world, most of which, if not all, predate young Vicks."

"Somewhat diluting her claim to the tontine, should it be established that Hadley died second," I concluded.

"Diluting? Positively spiking it, should one of Hadley's happy accidents happen to turn up on the doorstep."

"Do all of these artefacts come with a potential Tenpenny?" I asked, surveying a display case of what looked like tragically flawed table games.

"Not all, no." Lager joined me in examining a particularly mystifying device. "Paepae Kiori — Maori rat snare."

"Rat?" I asked.

"Hadley tells me it tastes like chicken."

"I believe I'll take his word for it. And this?"

"Inu blubber gun," said Lager. "Leverages the kinetic energy of frozen whale blubber to propel a whalebone harpoon with sufficient force to penetrate a whale. Employed, with a certain dark perpetuity, to hunt whales. Hadley traded a sledge team for it in Yellowknife. Said it saved his life in a standoff with Russian trappers in Rupert's Land. Have a look at this..."

Lager drew me across the room to an ornate vitrine mounted on the wall above the fireplace where, below decks, one would have found a likeness of a pre-adolescent Ratcliffe digging up the garden under the watchful eye of the nanny. Here however, were monsters.

"What the devil is it?" I asked of what appeared to me how I imagine internal organs look, or would, had I ever up until that moment imagined internal organs. The body, and I use that term loosely, was a translucent, inflated bladder, and from it dangled long, rangy tentacles, like some diabolical bagpipe, if that's not a tautology.

"Portuguese Man O'War," said Lager, with a tone suggesting that he was no more charmed by the display than was I. "Not a single creature at all, in fact, but something called a siphonophore. It's literally a community of tiny organisms working in harmony to torture little fish and give me nightmares. The tentacles are generously outfitted with venomous stingers which, I'm reliably informed, smart like billyo."

"I assume it tastes like chicken."

"Hadley regarded it as a sort of trophy, from what he described as a 'conquest' in the Aegean Sea, somewhere off Izmir." Lager repeated these details by rote, as stories he'd heard multiple times, and not as someone who could find Izmir on a map of Izmir.

"Conquest?" I asked. "Did Cousin Hadley invade Turkey?"

"Probably," said Lager. "But he didn't mean that sort of conquest. He was on a yacht with a party of English quality he'd met by chance on Mykonos. One of these society ladies fell overboard, it seems, while skeet-shooting, of all things. Once in the drink, a herd of these aberrants of nature converged on her and Hadley leapt into the middle of them, drawing their fire, as it were. Stung like the dickens, he said, and when he climbed aboard again this one was wrapped around his leg."

"Doesn't sound as much like a conquest, frankly, as it does a narrow escape."

"As indeed it was," agreed Lager. "That night, however, the lady in question was treating the stings with aniseed oil, when she found herself overcome with gratitude for Hadley's heroic sacrifice."

"Oh, that sort of conquest," I said. "A lady of standing, was she?"

"I expect so." Lager frowned and nodded sagely. "Forthcoming as the old man was — and frankly it was a task to get him to shut up, most of the time — this was one detail he refused to divulge. He'd only say that she was an English lady, and that I most certainly would be scandalised to know her name."

This was the sort of reveal normally accompanied by a thunderclap, or a collective 'oooo' from the audience. This intriguing morsel, however, was met with the mechanical clatter of a rotary doorbell, operated clumsily.

"That'll be Chancy," announced Lager. "He's coming

round with the deed to the tontine."

"Quick work. When did you tell him about the duel?"

"You know what? Strangest thing — I didn't." Lager led us back toward the lift as he spoke. "He sent us a wire — arrived sometime this afternoon — he knew about it already."

"Let us hasten to learn how... by stairs, I think, Lager," I suggested, in contemplation of another epic voyage through time. "Youth is but fleeting."

Lager went to fetch in the lawyer while I did the same for the law. I found Ivor still in place in the reading room, crouching over the suspicious artefacts.

"What do you make of this, then?" he asked as I poked my head through the door.

"Which?" I asked. "The blood stain or the discarded ramrod?"

"The curious coincidence of both." Ivor stood as he said this, still regarding the terrain like a particularly tricky sand hazard. "Plus blood on the index finger of this one."

"That would be Uncle Ratcliffe."

"Just so, Ratcliffe Tenpenny..." continued Ivor. "...blood on his hand, ramrod on the floor. Do you suppose he was trying to reload?"

"Unlikely," I surmised. "The box of powder and lead is on the mantelpiece. Not far, but a trying journey over difficult terrain for a man in a wheelchair. Assuming, of course, he actually needed a wheelchair."

"Do you have reason to doubt it?" Ivor had wandered

over to the fireplace and was examining the handsome pistol case.

"Not as such, no," I confessed. "Only the observation that both men, whose one shared interest was a decidedly twisted rivalry, acquired a similar affliction at about the same time in their lives."

"Are you planning on expanding on that, Mister Boisjoly, or must I ask?"

"Oh, yes, I'd forgotten that you arrived after the opening number," I recalled. "Ratcliffe and Hadley Tenpenny were the last remaining members of the beneficiary generation of an expiring family tontine. You know what a tontine is, I trust."

"Of course."

"Sort of an investment fund, set up by Tenpenny forefathers, to finance various industrial enterprises, railway charters to Canada, and whatnot."

"Thank you, Mister Boisjoly. I know what a tontine is."

"Of course," I said. "As did I, naturally. But this particular tontine was established in such a way which prevented it being liquidated until some later generation. The original investors and their heirs only ever received dividends, as a sort of bulwark against the dire risk of living a long life. No one could touch the fund itself, which is by now a king's ransom, until the second to last member of this generation had relinquished his claim in the only way allowable by law."

"So Ratcliffe and Hadley fought a duel so that at least one of them could enjoy the wealth of the tontine," concluded Ivor.

"So it would seem."

"Rather civilised," observed Ivor. "At least compared to some of the alternatives."

"I'm glad you said that, because I was thinking the same thing," I said. "But the very civility of the arrangement is what apparently marks it as sharply out of character for both men."

"And in any case, you're not having any of it," guessed Ivor.

"I'd be charmless without my native scepticism. I believe that for at least one of these men, the duel came as a complete surprise."

"Then how did they both come to be found dead behind a securely barricaded door?"

"Can't help thinking it's something to do with smoke," I said. "And possibly mirrors. This is the mystery aspect of the locked-room mystery, Inspector. We've already neatly established the first part of the equation — the room was locked. An optimist would say we're halfway home."

"What's the state of this tontine, then?" asked Ivor. "Who gets it now?"

"I believe that, according to the laws of the land, and if it can't be established which of these men died first, it's ritually scattered to the four winds." I confess, I was partially guessing at this. "Happily, I'm in a position to introduce you to someone who can expand on the finer points of law — Chauncey Proctor, the family solicitor, awaits us even now in the whisky room."

"The house has a whisky room?"

"Every room is a whisky room, with the right spirit," I said. "Doubtless Lager has found something with which to captivate the interests of a man of letters."

"I meant to ask — Lager?" asked Ivor.

"You mean why that, as opposed to, say, Lambic?"

"No, I mean as opposed to, say, his name."

"Oh, well, you know, when a clubmate has a name like Tenpenny, one feels rather obliged to decorate it with something cheaply had," I explained. "Then, in the ripeness of time, Tenpenny Lager becomes Lager Tenpenny, and laughs are roundly had."

"This passes for humour in the gentlemen's clubs of the nation, does it?"

"It may be largely in the telling," I admitted. "When Bergamot Peel tells it it's a hoot. Mind you, he has a lisp and a Hebredes accent."

Ivor hid his amusement behind a countenance of studied boredom.

"Did you say that the family solicitor was here?"

"Chauncy Proctor," I said. "We call him Chancy, though. Would you care to know the origin of that sobriquet, too?"

"I would not."

"Quite sure?" I asked. "It lacks the raucous etymology of the Lager story, but it's rather instructive."

"Quite sure."


The salon of number fifty-seven was like the other ground floor rooms, with yellowing walls and whittles of once-fashionable white, and dainty, dusty, disdained furnishings. Lager and Chancy were there, and they had neatly converted the space into a whisky room with the timely addition of a soda syphon and a bottle of the economical but serviceable Glen Glennegie '22 (before the introduction of copper purifiers to the distillery, but after the inevitably tragic experiment with clay casks).

"Help yourself, Anty," Lager said congenially but redundantly, as I busied myself with the sacred ritual of Scotch and syphon. "I'll take it that you're on duty, Inspector."

"Mister Proctor, I presume," Ivor said to the distinctly avian chap perched on a divan and holding his glass of whisky and soda as though he'd just won it in a spelling bee. Possibly the best way of describing Chancy Proctor is to observe that he resembles me, creased down the middle. Where I'm a bit tallish he's stretched, and where I'm thin he's narrow, so that the respective flanks appear just marginally too close together, most particularly his eyes. I understand he has to have his spectacles specially made with the lenses practically touching, and his attenuated, protruding beak completes the impression of a good-natured but easily startled songbird. As he was in the moment, Chancy usually sported a non-committal bit of a smile, like one does when one doesn't want to let on that one has failed to understand the joke.

"Pleased to meet you, Inspector," chirped Chancy. "Lager was just now telling me that the police have taken an interest in the affair."

"Indeed we have," confirmed Ivor. "Might I ask what brings you here today, of all days, Mister Proctor?"

"Well, I've come about the tontine, haven't I?" Chancy cast me a helpless sort of look.

"Cutting through the inevitable confusion, Inspector," I offered. "You should know that Chancy already knew about the duel."

"Might I know how that can be the case, Mister Proctor?" asked Ivor. "It's the view of Mister Boisjoly that not even both participants were aware that a duel was to occur."

"Oh, no, they were both signatories," said Chancy, rather cryptically, for those who know him — typically he's at his most enigmatic trying to recall the ingredients of his preferred tipple which, for the record, is just sherry. As he spoke, though, Chancy withdrew a weighty fold of paper from his breast pocket and held it out to Ivor, who tentatively took and opened it.

"What the devil is this?" he asked.

"A simple contract," explained Chancy, "in which both parties agree to settle the issue of the disposition of the Tenpenny Tontine by way of a duel, fought under governance of the Code Duello of 1777."

"Is this your signature as witness?" demanded Ivor.

"T'is," admitted Chancy, with a professional pride that suggested that he didn't realise that it was an admission at all. "It was all duly signed and sealed last Wednesday evening, over dinner." He leaned toward Lager, now, and spoke with a certain confidential awe. "We had Irish stew."

"You've known about this for nearly a week and you didn't think to inform the police or even the family?" asked Ivor, holding up the contract like it was exhibit A in Chancy's conviction for being an impenitent bean-brain.

"Ah, well, you see Inspector," Chancy spoke in his defence, "there's a little thing called legal professional privilege. I'm solicitor to both men, and it's not as though any laws were being broken."

"Except duelling," Ivor pointed out.

"That's not against the law, though, is it?" Then

Chancy's vacant smile broke and he looked at me. "Is it?"

"I thought you said this man was a solicitor," Ivor said to me.

"I offered to explain his nickname," I said. "You're not a famously capable solicitor, are you, Chancy?"

"Oh, my goodness." Chancy resumed smiling and giggled, and then leaned back into the divan with his drink. "No, not at all."

Ivor looked at me as he folded the contract in a worryingly meaningful fashion.

"Then that's the end of the matter," he said, handing the paper back to Chancy. "Apart, possibly, from arresting this imbecile for impersonating a solicitor."

Chancy received the document and smiled gamely at Ivor's fair analysis.

"Surely that's not the final word, Inspector," I said. "There's still at least one murder to be solved."

"Two murders, by the law of the land," corrected Ivor. "But both victims and perpetrators are dead, having left behind what amounts to a signed confession."

"Both what now?" stuttered Chancy.

"It's what I was telling you," explained Lager. "Uncle Ratcliffe and Cousin Hadley both died in the duel. Shot each other through the heart."

"What a singular thing,' said Chancy. "What becomes of the tontine, then?"

"That's rather what we were hoping you could tell us, Chancy old man," Lager replied with a little strain showing at the edges.

"Oh, yes, of course." Chancy pointed at himself and giggled at the thought. "Solicitor. Well, I suppose it comes down to which of them died first. With the death of either man the tontine is automatically dissolved in favour of he who remains. The entirety of the fund falls to his heirs."

"This is roughly what we assumed. What happens, though, if it can't be determined with any precision which of the men died first? We just divide it down the middle?" asked Lager.

"Oh, no. No, not at all." Chancy passed this verdict with uncharacteristic authority, and yet nodded his head. "Then the disposition of the tontine would fall to the jurisdiction of the Chancery Division of the High Court."

"And they'll just dole it out on a sort of, whatsit, order of merit, will they?" asked Lager.

"They'll award it to the state."

"The state?" Lager was accordingly aghast. "What's the state want with it? They've plenty of money. They literally print the stuff, don't they?"

"Nevertheless, it's effectively unclaimed."

"No it isn't. I claim it." Lager addressed all of us. "You're witnesses."

"I don't think you can do that, Lager." Chancy disagreed vaguely, while nodding firmly. "Look at what happened to poor Spigot."

"Spigot?" sputtered Lager. "What Spigot? Spigot what?"

"You remember," I reminded Lager. "Spigot Spoutswater-Smythe. He was a Juniper until he fell behind on his dues last year, poor chap. Rented Albert Hall for his great-uncle's wake, the late Lord Spinnaker, in anticipation of inheriting a not-insubstantial share of East-coast shipping, only to have his hopes dashed when the chancery upheld His Lordship's last will and testament, bequeathing everything — all but a royal appointment for live bait, I believe — to his parrot, and then awarding administration of the estate to the crown, on account of the parrot being judged feeble-minded."

"That's the chap," confirmed Chancy.

"What an appalling injustice," declared Lager.

"That was the view of the dailies at the time," I recalled. "Just because the poor creature couldn't speak for himself in court. Doubtless a case of nerves."

"I meant Spigot," corrected Lager, as though this should have been obvious.

"Oh, indeed, for him too," I agreed. "Last seen he was mudlarking for lugworm beneath Blackfriars Bridge."

"Right, I've heard enough," announced Ivor, with a tone that suggested the declaration was due sometime prior to the introduction of the parrot theme. "Mister Proctor, I'm sure I don't need to remind you…" he stopped, briefly, and took in Chancy's guileless good cheer, "…on second thought, I'm sure that I do need to remind you that you're in possession of evidence that will be required at the inquest, should the coroner choose to convene one."

"Evidence?" Chancy spoke the unfamiliar word with child-like curiosity.

"The contract, Mister Proctor," said Ivor, with poorly disguised impatience. "And of course the tontine itself."

"You can count on me, Inspector," declared Chancy, patting the pocket to which he'd returned the diabolical contract. "But, of course, I have no idea where the tontine papers are."

# CHAPTER SIX

# The Rarest Quirk of the Parish Clerk

"You don't mean to say you've gone and lost the deed to the tontine," exasperated Lager.

The inspector had left us to attend to what he described as 'things that actually matter', and Lager was now pressing the heretofore unknown case of the missing tontine.

"Of course I haven't lost it." Chancy took an indignant draw of his scotch and soda before adding, "I never had it."

"Chancy, of course you did," Lager reminded him. "It's been entrusted to your family firm for generations."

Chauncy the chancy lawyer shook his head and smiled knowingly. "It *was* entrusted to my family firm for generations. Terrence Tenpenny took it away from my grandfather in the 1880s, on account of a little mix-up involving some property deeds."

"Was that when the London office gave away most of Cap Ferrat to a man claiming to be Leopold II, king of the Belgians?" I asked.

"No, that was my father," Chancy recalled cheerfully.

"In his defence, he said the chap had a very convincing accent and a most intimidating beard."

"Devilishly clever."

"Infallibly so," agreed Chancy. "No, this was when my grandfather, acting in what he thought were the expressed interests of Sir Mannering Royce-Phipps, purchased at auction a hundred acres of bushland in the province of Victoria, in Australia."

"These were not the precise wishes of Sir Mannering?" I asked.

"Very nearly," said Chancy. "But what he actually wanted was to corner the market on development lands adjacent to Victoria Station — the one in London — before the expansion."

"Oh, dear."

"Yes. And Royce-Phipps had told my grandfather to go as high as five hundred pounds an acre."

"Oh, double dear." Then a peripheral thought struck me. "Sir Mannering Royce-Phipps was a founding member of the Juniper. That explains why you've been so definitively black-balled."

"Have I been blackballed from the Juniper?"

"The blackest," I assured him. "Positively raven. How could you not know? You've applied and been turned down eleven times."

"I assumed it was some sort of administrative error," said Chancy, uncertainly. Then he appeared to address a confidential aside to Lager, "They often happen, you know." Lager was only able to nod dumbly in reply.

"So, if you don't have the tontine," I asked, putting words to Lager's tortured expression, "where is it?"

"Right here."

"What do you mean, right here? Here in this room?"

"No. Well, possibly, I don't know. I only know that it's in this house," explained Chancy. "Sir Mannering and Terrence Tenpenny were acquaintances…"

"And Junipers," I added.

"Yes, indeed," acknowledged Chancy, somewhat ruefully. "After the Australia affair became known, Terrence Tenpenny withdrew his family's trust in our firm. He took charge of the tontine, personally, and hid it somewhere in this house. He left in our care only a cryptic clue to its whereabouts."

"Very well, Chancy, let's have it," said Lager. "Anty can figure it out, can't you Anty?"

"Modesty permits me to say only, probably."

Chancy put his drink ceremoniously on the side table, and then stood. He put his hands on his hips and looked skyward, as about to recite *Casabianca.* Then he looked downward with a sudden frown.

"Oh, I say. I've forgotten it."

"Read it out then, Chancy," demanded Lager. "Unless you mean to tell us that your family has raised the standard of incompetence to the level of committing such a vital piece of information to your so-called memory."

"Oh, no, it's written down," said Chancy. "I just didn't think to bring it with me."

"Didn't think to bring it with you?"

"I assumed I'd remember it."

"You must recall some of it, Chancy," encouraged Lager, like the off-stage director of a Christmas play performed by idiot children. "Anty can figure it out, can't you Anty?"

"Modesty begins to play hardball, I fear, Lager," I admitted. "Cryptic messages tend to need reading in their entirety. It's rather integral to their nature. In any case, time marches on, and it's enough, for now, to know that the tontine is safely stored on the premises. The more pressing matter is murder."

"I thought that was all settled," said Lager.

"On the contrary, my dear Lager, the matter is very much unsettled." I returned my glass to its tray and twirled my hat, two universally recognised preliminaries to imminent departure. "Inspector Wittersham must be convinced, as I thoroughly am, that a third party was implicit in today's tragic events."

"But, the contract," countered Chancy.

"A mere setback, Chancy old thing," I countered right back. "Possibly even a clue unto itself. Your job — and you might want to write this down — is to fetch the cryptic message and return it safely here. Lager, you'll need to show some of that gentlemanly restraint for which we Junipers are famous, and resist the urge to tear the house apart looking for the tontine. We'll sort it out when I return."

"Where are you going?" asked Lager.

"In the immediate term, Kensington, ancient land of my people," I answered. "But when you next see me I hope to have a fuller picture of what drove two civilised men of a certain age to such desperate measures."

"I think we know, already, Anty," said Lager. "It was the tontine."

"Probably so," I agreed. "Nevertheless, I feel there's a good deal more to this whole affair than the probable. In any case, Lager old clubmate, it strikes me that the most immediate issue is the tontine itself, and preserving it in Tenpenny hands."

ॐ

Gutter Folly is one of those meandering, wavy sort of towns installed inland along one of Essex's less hard-working tributaries to the English Channel. It's the sort of community established in the days when there was some sort of industry to be made of marshlands and stagnant waters. Mud, I suppose, back when there was a shortage. The train station was built on the last stretch of solid ground and consequently a good ten miles from the scattered, hewn-stone cottages, tumble-down churches, squat pubs of a maritime theme named 'The Snail' or 'The Herring' or 'The Snail and Herring', and numerous, idle swamps, teeming with flying insects and the amphibians who love them. The omnibus journey from London, with a change at Chelmsford, took just over an hour. It took nearly another two, counting waiting for the taxi driver to finish his shift as stationmaster, to achieve downtown Gutter Folly.

The town is perhaps ten miles square in high heels but its only road is such a serpentine knot through the jungles of coastal Essex that, stretched out, it would probably reach the moon. There was no high street, as such, discounting a bait shop that also did tea, and a good fifteen twisting minutes later we'd arrived at St Barnabas, the Parish Church of Gutter Folly. I could still see the bait shop.

All good station-master-cum-cabbies worth their whistle and cloth cap will know where to find just about anything there is to find in a town the size of Gutter Folly and my driver, one Sullivan 'Stick Shift' Southey, needed only to hear the words 'Parish Clerk' and there I was. The parish church of St Barnabas confronts all visitors with a square tower of gently crumbling layers of blue lias, like an immense *mille feuilles* topped with ramparts and crosses. The rest of the church is probably a bit newer, perhaps a mere five hundred years old, and composed of rough sandstone block with carved granite ornamentation. The sort of solid old English aesthetic best viewed under cloudy skies with foggy patches and a seventy percent chance of precipitation, so the scene was laid out picture-perfect.

The church grounds were an unkempt patchwork of sand and cemetery and there were weeds growing through the steps to the front door. A footpath showing signs of marginally more traffic to the apse entrance suggested to me that this was the way to the parish clerk's office. That, and the sign that said 'This way to the Parish Clerk's office.'

There's a dangerous radicalism present in all parish clerk's offices, it seems to me, what with a portrait of King George on one wall facing down a crucifix on the other, in stern, silent testament to the conflicting loyalties of the place of worship which also serves as the county records office. This one was no different, in that respect, nor in the dense, disused dustiness of the place. In another regard, though, it was unlike any parish clerk's office I'd ever seen or imagined, in all my years of imagining them.

The only furniture to speak of was a small desk and chair and there was nothing on the desk at all except a pair of well-worn workbooks. Behind the boots was a newspaper which lowered with a snap as I opened the door, and behind that was of all things a girl.

"Blimey," she said, wide-eyed. "A customer."

She took her feet off the desk and rose to an absolute corker of country womanhood. Her face was round and pinched and cherry-cheeked in that impossible way that manages to be both adorable and alluring in equal measure. The theme continued down the rest of her, which weaved in and out like a Gutter Folly freeway, highlighted quite definitively by a work shirt and a pair of dungarees pulled tight at the waist with a man's belt which could have gone round a second time. Her blonde hair was a delightfully insouciant mess, as though she and it were content to allow one another to live their own lives.

"Oh, I say," I seem to have uttered.

"Hello."

"Ehm, parish clerk?"

"Hello again," she said, holding out a hand. "Quiescence Keats. Mister...?"

"Ha," I laughed. "I knew it a second ago." I shook her hand. "It all comes rushing back, now. Anthony Boisjoly. Simpler if you call me Anthony or, later, when confiding to your private diary the moment our eyes first met, Anty."

"My friends call me Quip."

"Do they?"

"Beats Quiescence."

"Positively leaves it standing at the post," I concurred. "Quip it is, then. What an original form of cruelty."

"I think my parents hoped that the name would infuse in me qualities desirable in a wife, in their antediluvian view — it was between 'Quiescence' and 'Doormat'."

"Close run thing."

"Well, I'd very much like to stand here talking about me all day..."

"So would I," I agreed, looking around the room, "but I'd prefer to sit."

"I'm sure you didn't come here just to talk to me."

"Not initially, no. I came to enquire with the parish clerk, but that seems so mundane a pursuit, now."

"I am the parish clerk, Anty." Quip drew my attention to a folding chair by the door, and we took our respective places on either side of the desk.

"Isn't that a role normally played by an eager young curate, seeing out his journeyman years in quiet service until he can lay hands on a lucrative vicarage and really start raking in the souls?"

Quip nodded. "We completely ran out of eager young curates, 'round the same time the local industry dried up."

"I was going to ask about that," I said. "Well, no, frankly, I wasn't, but now you've introduced the theme, what local industry?"

"Smuggling, mainly." Quip gazed with nostalgia at some reminiscence hovering over my left shoulder. "For a brief, incandescent period in its history, Gutter Folly was the epicentre of trade for most of the Belgian chocolate consumed in the South-East, and we sold more Turkish tobacco into London than all legal channels combined." She said all this with a sort of dreamy caprice, as I'm told Napoleon would often reflect with soft whimsy on his exile to the island of Elba, from imprisonment on the barren rock of St Helena.

"That's almost the last thing I might have guessed," I said. "I had formed the view that the local economy was based largely on frogs and, I don't know, algae, or something."

"Because of the marshes."

"Just so, because of the marshes," I confirmed. "You do have rather a lot of them."

"They're salt marshes, the only lasting byproduct of the folly which gave the town its name."

"Gutter Folly wasn't named for the famous cartographers and explorers of the Essex interior, Messrs Gutter and Folly?"

"It was called Drab-on-Drabble," replied Quip, with a flat, 'could be worse' smile and inflexion. "Until an ambitious engineering effort to irrigate the otherwise infertile lands by means of a channel from the river."

"That would be the gutter bit," I conjectured. "And the folly?"

"Dug in the wrong direction entirely, starting too close to the mouth of the river. Ended up saturating the land for miles with seawater," explained Quip. "What started as an honest and even high-minded effort to irrigate dry lands ended as a literal salting of the earth."

"How biblical," I said. "Couldn't they just fill it in?"

"Could have done, I suppose, had there been the will... and the budget... and any farmers in Drab-on-Drabble to fill it in for." Quip ceased her glance into the past, now, and instead looked directly at me, and I found myself adjusting my tie, as one does, and picturing her in a wedding gown. "In any case, ineffective as it was at irrigation, the gutter did bring a whole new industry to the town."

"The aforementioned trade in duty-free imports, you mean."

"For perhaps obvious reasons, the gutter never made it onto any nautical maps. It was literally a hidden harbour with easy access to the Channel, not to mention dozens of marshes at the bottom of which, to this day, no doubt, are hidden thousands of bottles of French wine and brandy."

"Apropos of nothing at all," I said, "do you know where I can rent a boat?"

Quip smiled at this with full, naturally ruby lips at which da Vinci would have downed tools in despair. "Probably not worth the bother. Anyway, if it's smuggled brandy you're after, the industry's not completely gone. It's just most of the practitioners have retired to private life. My father is, as we speak, somewhere in the Charentais, negotiating a shipment of armagnac."

"Oh yes?" Now reminded that, of course, this girl must have parents, I found myself thinking of ways in which I might curry favour with them. "Put me down for the lot. Will he be back soon?"

"Probably not. It takes time to arrange backhanders, even with the French."

"Don't I know it. I once spent two hours and the equivalent of nearly five pounds just to organise a pumpkin that I could drop off a second-floor balcony of Le Crillon Hotel onto Place de la Concorde. Even then I had to settle for a cantaloupe which, doubtless you know, is hardly the same effect at all. When do you expect your father back?"

"July."

"That's probably not going to work," I said, looking at my watch. "Last train back to London is the 18:41. And your mother?"

"Ran off with a customs inspector before the war."

"I'm not surprised," I said. "Dashing devils."

"I think it was more down to my father spending most of his time on the continent. He's rarely home. A woman likes to know where her husband is, and for that to be, from time to time, home, or at the very least a nearby prison."

"Now, I simply cannot understand chaps like that," I said. "Me, I'm quite the opposite. Nothing I like more than spending time at home or in a nearby prison, just, you know, making my whereabouts known to loved ones at all times."

"I gather home is in London."

"Kensington, to be pretentiously accurate," I said. "You'll like it there. Almost no swamps at all, apart from some squishy bits of Holland Park, should you grow nostalgic for home."

"Not for me," said Quip, shaking her head and auguring the first fissures in our affair. "Can't bear London."

I was speechless, of course, as would have been any right-thinking individual.

"I... see," I finally said. The mists began to clear and I recalled something about a tontine. "Ratcliffe Tenpenny, né Coleridge, 1859."

"You're looking for a birth certificate?"

"Don't you have any?"

"Thousands." Quip nodded. I flatter myself that she disliked this shift onto professional terms as much as I did. "What's your interest in this particular specimen?"

"Frankly, I'm very much hoping to discover that there's something subtly swindly about it," I said. "I expect you get this sort of thing all the time."

"Not in recent memory. What is the nature of this dodginess you suspect?"

"Well, nothing very particular," I confessed. "It's just that the birth certificate or, more precisely, a subsequent amendment thereof, positions the subject as the beneficiary to a very substantial inheritance."

"And you're the hero who's going to save him from the temptations of wealth," speculated Quip.

"Ah, no. It's marginally more complicated than that," I said. "And when I say marginally, I mean exponentially. You see, Mr Tenpenny né Coleridge has passed on, and by an extraordinary confluence of circumstances, unless it is shown that either he or his rival for the fortune is not a legitimate heir, then the whole lot goes to the crown."

"Couldn't they just come to some sort of arrangement?"

"An attempt was made," I said.

"That's all you need? The birth certificate?"

"I'll take anything you've got, if there's a volume discount," I said. "What have you, besides birth certificates? Is there a catalogue I might look at?"

"It's the parish records office — we've got it all. Your entire life story is in our files, birth certificate, christening, smallpox vaccine if you were born after 1853 when it became mandatory, marriage if you got married, incarceration if you've had any sort of fun at all, and, inevitably, your death certificate."

"No wonder you ran out of eager young curates," I observed. "What about end of term reports and ill-advised missives left on the pillow of the downstairs maid?"

"No, nothing like that."

"That's certainly a relief," I said. "Shall we have a look, then?"

I watched with soft regret for what might have been as Quip twirled out of her chair like the inspiration for the very first snowflake and disappeared behind an unmarked door. I entertained myself with hopes that, upon her return, she'd say something akin to 'Oh, *London* — I thought you said Frinton-on-Sea. Can't stick Frinton-on-Sea, but London...'

No such luck, though. When she eventually returned she was merely shuffling and studying several sheets of ageing certificate paper.

"Sorry that took so long — there was something of a run on baby boys in 1859." She put the papers on the desk. "There you go, Ratcliffe Coleridge, June 12, 1859." She turned the birth certificate right way round for me. "Amended, August 12, 1881, to identify the father as one Terrence Tenpenny."

"Yes," I said, studying the document. "Yes, most intriguing."

"What do you see?"

"Frankly, nothing at all. Seems entirely correct, to my admittedly untrained eye."

"What were you hoping to find?" Quip leaned over the desk on both elbows, as I was doing, and when I looked up we were intimately eye-to-eye.

"Not sure." This came out rather hoarsely, for some reason, and I cleared my throat. "A telling misspelling, for instance, or evidence of the use of a ballpoint pen."

"It's legitimate," adjudged Quip, refocusing demurely on the birth certificate.

"How can you tell?"

"The signatures." Quip put a shapely finger on the endorsement of certification of birth. "The Reverend Merrion Davidy Lloyd, rector of St Barnabas for over forty years."

"Rather an involved autograph," I observed of the whirl of swirls and flourishes with which Davidy Lloyd had signed the birth certificate. It put me in mind of a nautical map of the currents and trade winds that so vex shipping off the Horn of Africa. "It's a wonder he had time for anything else."

"He found a moment to sign the amendment." Quip pointed out that, indeed, Davidy Lloyd had stamped his irksomely inimitable signature over a note which transferred paternity from, of all people, Samuel Taylor Coleridge, to Terrence Tenpenny.

I found myself suddenly remembering a snatch of pertinent prose, and I let fly...

*"My hopes are with the dead, anon*
*My place with them will be,*
*And I with them shall travel on*
*Through all futurity*
*Yet leaving here a name, I trust,*
*That will not perish in the dust."*

Quip smiled at me the way one smiles at children who've managed to tie their shoes.

"Coleridge?"

"Robert Southey," I said. "I note that the station master's surname is also Southey. So, by no coincidence, is that of the driver of the station taxi. Coleridge, Southey…"

"Well spotted," said Quip. "Yes, the entire village is composed almost exclusively of Shelleys, Blakes, Byrons, and Wordsworths."

"How… novel?"

"Davidy Lloyd had a pronounced weakness for the Romantic poets," explained Quip.

"So, it would seem, did the women of Gutter Folly," I observed.

"I think it was a rudimentary inventory system of the reverend's own invention."

"Inventory? Inventory of what?"

"More like an accounting method," corrected Quip reflectively, "for Gutter Folly's second most prolific industry — really, rather a byproduct of the first — illegitimate children."

"Big market for that sort of thing, is there?" I asked.

"Plenty of supply, anyway, when most of the men in the village are effectively itinerant pirates."

"And the Reverend Davidy Lloyd obliged with forged birth certificates," I said. "Decidedly broad-minded, in my experience of Victorian-era rectors."

"His views were famously aligned with those of the Romantics he admired," explained Quip. "He was once reprimanded by the Bishop of Rochester for basing an entire St Martin's Day homily on Cantos five through sixteen of Byron's *Don Juan.*"

"Even fifteen?" I asked.

"Especially fifteen."

"Blimey," I said, and I meant it. "So, the reverend was happily distributing romantic poets on a rotation basis to children who would otherwise grow up with the stain of illegitimacy."

"In a nutshell."

"It's no wonder Terrence Tenpenny ensconced his shame in Gutter Folly — what better place to hide an illegitimate heir than a village of bastard Blakes and Byrons." I shifted the birth certificate to reveal the only other documentary evidence of Ratcliffe Tenpenny's wild youth. "What's this then?"

"Baptismal certificate." Quip started to turn the document to face me but then quickly snatched it up. "Hello, that's a coincidence."

"What is?" I asked. "Is the godfather Percy Bysshe Shelley?"

"No, but the godmother is none other than Willow Willoughby." Quip turned around the document so I could see it.

"I'm unfamiliar with her work," I confessed. "One of the later subjectivists?"

"My grandmother. She would have been the boy's nanny."

"That is a coincidence," I agreed. "Did she ever mention Ratcliffe Coleridge?"

"Maybe. I'm not sure I would have made the connection. We know rather a lot of people named Coleridge."

"Yes, I daresay you do," I said. "Pity I can't talk to your grandmother — she might have had insights into another, tangential matter."

"Why can't you talk to my grandmother? She's very nice."

"You don't mean to tell me that Willow Willoughby is still with us," I said. "She must be ninety years old."

"Of course she isn't ninety years old," scolded Quip. "How old do you think I am?"

"I'd have guessed my age, give or take," I equivocated, "but if Willow Willoughby was nanny to Ratcliffe Tenpenny, who must have been in his seventies up until yesterday, when he became timeless, then that would make her, approximately, quite old."

"My nan had my father when she was eighteen, as was the fashion of the time, and he had me when he was fifty, because he was otherwise indisposed. Nan's nowhere near ninety years old."

"How old is she?"

"Eighty-eight."

"And does she still live here in Gutter Folly?" I asked, hoping for something but, at the time, I knew not what.

"Mhmm." Quip nodded. "At a crumbling pile called Drab House."

"To this day?" I marvelled. "I've seen photographs of your grandmother with her charge on the grounds of the place. You don't suppose she'd receive me were I to visit, do you?"

"I don't see why not," said Quip, casting an appraising eye over me. "Drab House isn't really the centre of the social cyclone it was in the day. Like the village and, for that matter, Nan and me, the place is badly underfunded. If you could nail down a couple of stairs or retile the roof while you're there, it would be very much appreciated."

I paid for and arranged copies of the certificates to be delivered to Lager, if only as a souvenir of my first failed effort to rule out one of the rivals for the Tenpenny Tontine, and bade my regretful farewells.

# CHAPTER SEVEN

# Stow's Surprising Secret Side

Stick-shift Southey, stoutly reliable as he'd been all throughout our acquaintance, was waiting patiently to return me to the station, asleep in the back of his taxi. New arrangements were made, and within minutes we were twisting out of a thick spinney of wooded wetland and into view of the earthly remains of the baroque manor house that I'd seen in photographs on Ratcliffe Tenpenny's mantlepiece.

The years, as is so often euphemistically said, had not been kind. In the case of Drab House, in fact, the years had been nothing short of sadistic. The grounds, which in the pictures I'd seen had been snipped and symmetrical and systematically topiaried, were now a broad field of dry, waving weeds, sagging, diseased hardwoods, and a fallow deer. The house itself still had its Roman columns topped with cherubs, impossibly tall, stone-framed windows, and a multiplicity of turrets and towers. However, the majority of the cherubs had lost at least one wing and many were missing other essential bits. A good half the windows were boarded up and the other half probably should have been. The plaster of the columns was cracked and falling away, like the icing on Miss Havisham's famous wedding cake, and countless barn swallows flitted gaily in and out of numerous holes in the roof. Finally but most conspicuously, part of the natural rising on which the house had been built had, at some point, slid away, taking the entire northeast tower along for the ride.

"People live here?" I said incredulously to Stick-shift as he manoeuvred us gently through a labyrinth of creeping thistle and dandelion higher and, quite possibly, older than the car.

"Everyone does," answered Stick-shift, somewhat mysteriously, I thought at the time. "Expect to see out *my* days here, when the time comes."

"Do you? For what crime?"

"Same one of which we're all one day guilty," he said, equally mysteriously. "Getting old."


I felt very much as Doctor Livingstone might have felt upon discovering the source of the Nile, had he done so, when we broke free of the bracken and into a barren clearing before the perilously sagging front steps of Drab House. There, I bade the station-master-cum-taxi-driver-cum-cryptic-philosopher stand by yet again for his long-anticipated opportunity to deliver me to the train.

The double oak doors had been divided into six distinct panels by long and deep cracks but they stood open in that firm, swollen way of doors that can't be closed. I let myself in.

The foyer was a deep and wide hall, perhaps occupying half of the width of the house and all of its depth. In the tradition of rich, baroque interiors it was generously ornamented in gold leaf and it had an elaborate fresco on the high ceiling. In the tradition of neglected ruins, the gold had been mostly peeled away and the fresco — a rococo oil in perspective of tall pines and a blue sky, designed to give the impression of looking up from a forest floor — had withered and chipped and faded and now gave the impression of looking up from the bottom of a compost heap.

Once past the peeling walls and threadbare tapestry and imminent collapse, though, there was something rather clubby about the great room, in that it was populated by clubmen. Distributed about the place on divans with split upholstery and lounge chairs decorated with plumes of breakaway cotton stuffing were gentlemen of a certain age, smoking cigars and drinking brandy and playing cards, in a tableau reminiscent of my own Juniper Gentleman's Club — the key difference being that most of these chaps were awake at four o'clock in the afternoon.

Two such specimens with thinning hair and thickening waistcoats eyed me circumspectly from a makeshift cribbage board formed of hat pins and an ageing copy of *Jude the Obscure.*

"Oy," spoke the thinner, trimmer chap on the left. Having locked in my attention, he squinted in all directions before lowering his voice and asking, "Got any cigarettes?"

"No, sorry, I don't," I said.

"Want to buy some?" asked the rounder, redder, more generously moustachioed of the pair.

"Do you a deal on five thousand Dutch blend, pre-rolled," added Thinner, with whispered benevolence.

"That's awfully kind of you," I said. "I'm frankly not sure what I'd do with five thousand cigarettes, especially once they'd already been rolled."

"Sell them on, obviously," said Redder.

"You'll want to be quick about it, too," added Thinner. "Some of them are getting a bit mouldy."

"You're beguiling salesmen," I admitted, "but I must nevertheless find the strength to refuse. I'm actually here on a social call — can either of you direct me to Willow Willoughby?"

The men shared a meaningful glance across the Thomas Hardy cribbage board.

"She's not really here," said Thinner.

"Isn't she?" I asked. "I have it from a source quite close to the subject that Mrs Willoughby rarely if ever leaves Drab House."

"She's here, you understand," clarified Redder. Or, at least, he sounded as though he thought he was clearing things up. To me, it seemed that the gentlemen were speaking very much at cross-purposes. "She's just not entirely here, if you take my meaning."

"Perhaps you could just point me toward the portion that is here, then."

"Ladies normally take to Drab Gallery, this time of day," said Thinner, pointing with a nod to a hall exiting from the back left of the foyer.

"Thank you very much," I said. "Out of curiosity, where is the rest of Mrs Willoughby?"

"1867," answered Redder, turning back to his game. "Give or take."


Drab Gallery was a long hall occupying the back of the house, giving it a choice view of the swamp and beyond that, glimmering grey and greyer, the river Drabble. The exterior wall was composed of floor-to-ceiling windows and the windows were composed mainly of cracked, foggy panes of glass. The interior wall was a gallery of discoloured rectangles on the yellow striped, yellow wallpaper where once paintings had hung. Dotted along the corridor beneath the wall of absent portraits and, I suppose, the occasional absent landscape, were a dozen or so elderly ladies practising the traditional trades of their species — crocheting, knitting, needlepointing, and fostering what looked a lively market in lurid gossip. I instantly became the subject of squinting scrutiny and much murmuring.

I scanned the jury for a likely guide but in a moment I'd isolated the elusive Willow Willoughby from a broad field of likely suspects. None of the ladies were in the bloom of youth but only one of them could have been nearing ninety and passing the lion's share of her day in the Victorian era.

Quip's grandmother wore a once-whitish pinafore apron over a once-stylish mauve number with a high collar and strangulatory bodice. Her hair was completely silver, but that particular shade of silver that you get from slowly ageing walnut-coloured hair, and it fell over her shoulder in a long braid. Her face was round and cheery and the hilly topology of her bodice foretold of many years of robust making-men-forget-what-they-were-thinking-about for her granddaughter.

She sat at a small, ornate, *écritoire* and chewed thoughtfully on the end of a fountain pen and sought her muse in the swamp beyond the window. In the moment the swamp provided, and she seemed very happy with the contribution — she dipped her pen in the inkwell and continued her letter.

"Mrs Willoughby?" I said, once I was in hailing distance.

"Ah, Stow, there you are." The old woman looked kind familiarity at me over her reading glasses. "I'll have some letters shortly for you to post."

I was left unsure how to reply to this — I'd been assured already that the senior Willoughby was batty as a two-century inning; perhaps if I corrected the subtle error — for all I knew this Stow chap and I were as alike as Jacob and Esau — I might provoke a collision with reality from which Quip's nan might never recover. On the other hand, it would be awkward to pose searching questions to someone who thinks I'm the butler.

It was the action which the dowager Willoughby performed next that tipped the scales. After giving me fair warning about my impending duties, re the post office, she once again dipped her pen in the inkpot and continued writing with buoyant inspiration, and all this drew my attention to the clear fact that she had run out of ink probably before the turn of the last century, and she was scratching spotlessly onto a sheet of blank paper.

"Very good, madam," I said. It was obviously not within the scope of my duties to disturb the nanny while she composed her correspondence, so I passed the time taking in the other eccentricities on her writing desk. There was a stack of post, as advertised, formed of stuffed envelopes with neither addresses nor stamps. Scattered about the desk and its shelves was blotting paper, spare nibs, an abused address book, and many pictures, all of which I'd seen before on Ratcliffe Tenpenny's mantelpiece, but with the distinction that none of them showed him any older than, at most, ten years old.

"What's another good word for 'synonym', Stow?" asked Mrs Willoughby, her brow furrowed in thought. "I've already used it once in this paragraph."

"Metonym?"

"Hmmm." Grandma Willoughby carefully reread the entire letter, up to the point where she needed another word for 'synonym'. "I'll just use 'equivalent'," she said, and then lowered her voice to confidentially share, "Between you, me, and Vicky," she made nodding reference to a substantial faded spot on the wall under which gleamed a plaque reading 'HRM Victoria', "his lordship isn't among our more literary correspondents. In his most recent letter he spelt 'proud' with a 'w'... and an 'e', now I think of it."

She busied herself again with her dry pen, finished the document, signed and carefully blotted it, and then folded it into an envelope. She placed the blank envelope, which had evidently been addressed earlier, onto the stack, which she then handed to me.

"See if you can't make the afternoon post, Stow," she said. "I've been terribly remiss, lately. I haven't written Bishop Cooley since before end of term, and I completely forgot to send condolences to poor Sir Bromley Baker when his uncle was eaten in Fiji."

"Certainly madame," I assured her. "I'll see to it straight away."

"Oh, dear me." Mrs Willoughby was examining the loose leaves of the shedding address book. "Stow, is there an envelope addressed to Tobias Lord Trilby?"

"Ehm." I sorted through the blank envelopes. Presumably the safest answer was, "Yes, here it is. Lord Trilby."

"And what address have I put for old Topsy?"

"Ehm," I said again, for it still seemed fresh and fit for purpose. I endeavoured to slide an eye over the address book in Mrs Willoughby's hand, and I did so, but the faded hieroglyphics on the yellow sheets were the opposite of meaningful. "Flattery Hall…" I said, struggling to make something of what I could see of the book and miming reading the address from the envelope. "…Nutty, Smoked Ham? No, that'll be Netley, Southampton, of course… ehm…"

Finally, I turned the envelope around so that Nanny Willoughby could read it herself. Instead, she looked at me as if she barely recognised the faithful Stow.

"That is addressed to Mister Tenpenny," she said at last, and held out her hand that I might give her the stack of envelopes.

"Ha, of course, so it is," I said and, picking up on the deeply disguised opportunity, asked, "Will Miss Halisham-Lewes have anything for me to post, madam?"

"The boy's mother is still on the continent, Stow," said Mrs Willoughby, as she set about assuring that Lord Trilby's missive was correctly addressed. "You remember — we had her seeing-off do only last week. You tried to dance to *Kalinka* while simultaneously playing it on the piano."

I was starting to like this Stow chap.

"Ah, yes, of course. When might we enjoy another such *soirée,* do you suppose? I've been working on a right-handed version of *Flying Trapeze* which frees my left to twirl a baton in time."

"A boy needs his mother, of course," said the loving nanny. "Miss Halisham-Lewes won't be back any later than 1871."

# CHAPTER EIGHT

# The Vintage Vantage of Vickers

Vickers, Boisjoly family heirloom and personal valet, was in the front salon when I returned to the Kensington manor, laying out tea.

"I'm back, Vickers," I said, dropping into an armchair and bouncing my feet up onto a strategically-placed occasional which had grown accustomed to the abuse. "Just a whisky and soda, if you don't mind."

"But, it's tea-time, sir," said Vickers, with the same sort of firm, admonishing tone he would employ when I was a child and he was my father's valet, catching me pouring a couple of fingers of Papa's best brandy into my porridge.

"It's just gone midnight, actually," I gently corrected. "And we have more pressing matters than tea. What do you know of a town called Gutter Folly?"

"Very little, I fear." This was typically a good sign. Vickers was of the aged and elongated variety of valet, like a saged cyprus in goldfinch waistcoat, and while he looked about ninety years old it was broadly assumed that he was much older. He had begun jettisoning excess ballast — such as all notion of time and three-dimensional space — as we neared the end of the reign of Queen Victoria, but his capacity for retention of all that he'd learned up until then was beyond reproach. "I can only think of the infamous rector of the village, the Reverend Merrion Davidy Lloyd."

"Put the place on the map with a rousing homily on the moral guidance to be found in Byron's Don Juan, I understand," I added.

"Yes, sir." Vickers spilt the perfect minimum of soda into a glass of whisky and handed it duly over. "He also, I believe, achieved some sort of record for longest-serving rector of a parish town without a charter, bridge, or historic battlefield."

"Is that an accomplishment?" I asked. "I've seen Gutter Folly — not really the sort of place I'd want to be rectoring or doing much of anything else for forty years."

"Indeed, sir. I believe the appointment and duration thereof was seen as largely punitive."

"Ah, that makes more sense." I took a meditative draw on my whisky-and-distraction-from-whisky. "What about smuggling?"

"As you have already observed, sir, it's getting late."

"I meant with respect to Gutter Folly," I clarified. "Was there ever any talk of covert activities?"

"Not to my knowledge, no, but of course by the very nature of activities which are covert, it is likely they would have escaped my notice."

"Yes, good point," I conceded. "That's all largely in the past now, in any case, apart from a promising junket to the Charentais — we may need to reorganise the cellar at short notice, incidentally — most of the practitioners appear to be living in what amounts to a retirement home for ageing smugglers."

"This is very gratifying to hear, sir."

"Only because you haven't heard all of it," I said. "The residence in question is less a retirement 'home' and more a retirement 'pile of cracked plaster and rotting timber'. There's a fallow deer living on the grounds and a small but spirited community of bats hanging from the chandelier in the dining room."

"Most disturbing," said Vickers. "I was wondering, if it's not taking a liberty..."

"Not at all, Vickers. I would have nothing come between us, apart from a thousand years of feudal tradition, obviously. Speak your mind."

"Why are we discussing Gutter Folly?"

"A choice question, Vickers, I recommend it highly, for it opens the door to much intrigue. Have I ever mentioned a fellow Juniper name of Tenpenny?"

"Tenpenny..." Vickers said the name wistfully, as though for him it evoked distant memories of tall ships and dangerous ports of call.

"No matter," I continued. "It's enough to know, for the moment, that this chap's uncle Ratcliffe has been killed in a duel during which both parties expired."

"How very singular," observed Vickers.

"Isn't it? You'd think this sort of thing would happen all the time, given the logistics of the game, but apparently it's quite novel. What's more, it's not what actually happened. Both men died instantly, but the shots were heard several seconds apart."

"There was a third party."

"There was, indeed, a third party," I agreed. "The problem that presents, however, is predicated on another noteworthy fact of the affair — the duel was fought behind securely locked doors."

"A phenomenon which has become your rather dubious speciality," said Vickers.

"Which is why I was called in," I continued. "A fortune lies in the balance, the value of which far exceeds the dreams of avarice. Indeed, by all accounts it laughs derisively at the paltry dreams of avarice. But unless it can be established which of the men died first, the state lays claim to every last bauble and button."

"I believe I'm beginning to understand the gravity of the situation." Vickers had begun wandering the room at a certain point, as is his habit when listening or not listening, as the case may be, and was now pouring himself a cup of the tea he'd prepared for me. "To keep the fortune in the hands of the family you must determine which of the two men was murdered."

"That would seem the way forward, but there's a complication," I said. "Several complications, in fact. Firstly the mystery is, for the moment, impenetrable. All four chief — but by no means only — suspects were a verifiable distance from the events when they occurred. All four were in each other's company when access to the room was finally achieved, and all four can confirm that both men were dead, ostensibly, by the other's hand."

"In my own very direct experience, sir, you've bested more obtuse conundrums."

"Your confidence is appreciated and, if it's not being uncharacteristically immodest, well-placed," I said. "However the second obstacle to solving this crime is that, from the perspective of the police, made manifest in our old friend Inspector Ivor Wittersham, there is no crime to solve — the victims signed a document agreeing to shoot at each other until one of them was rich. Rather neatly scuppers my initial suggestion that the duel was a ruse."

"What an extraordinary measure," commented Vickers. "Is such a contract legal?"

"Probably not, but it's certainly enough to grant a bureaucrat like Wittersham cause to return to his banal bank robberies and routine cases of obtaining goods or services by deception."

"Surely that can't have been the intended purpose of the arrangement," said Vickers. "More tea, sir?"

"Please." I handed Vickers my glass and he set about it with bottle and syphon. "There's a tiny, isolated portion of Pimlico where the absence of familiarity with the laws of the land regarding duelling is nothing short of astonishing. The purpose of the document was, in theory, to afford legal protection to the surviving party. The two men hated each other, you see, and this was the most civilised solution to the pressing problem of the tontine that they could manage."

"I take it, then, that your most immediate objective is to establish that a crime was committed." Vickers returned my glass in a much more respectable state than that in which he found it.

"A very worthy guess, Vickers, but no," I said. "I have no avenues of inquiry in that line, for the moment, and in any case the more pressing matter is stewardship of the tontine itself. There's no obvious way of determining which of the men died first and without such a determination the entire fortune will go to the state, who'll doubtless just piffle it away on another war or royal wedding or some such inconsequential frivolity."

"It's difficult to see what else might be done," said

Vickers.

"That's because you're drinking tea, my dear Vickers. An excellent accompaniment to scones and cucumber sandwiches, no sane man would ever dispute that, but of less than no help at all when looking for the side-entrance to a quandary. For that, nothing short of the finest barley oil will serve." To demonstrate the distinction, I took a restorative draw on my whisky-and-whatsit. "Which brings us, fully and finally, to Gutter Folly. I went there to look at a birth certificate."

"Have they especially interesting examples of the genre in Gutter Folly?" asked Vickers.

"They do, in fact, signed by none other than the ribald reverend himself, "I said. "I was in town tacking the course of legitimacy. There are some not inconsiderable grounds to believe that at least one of the deceased didn't have a legal claim on the tontine, which would mean that regardless of who died first, the fortune would remain in Tenpenny hands."

"Tenpenny…" mused Vickers, again appearing to gaze dreamily down the corridors of time.

"The name starting to ring a familiar tune, is it?"

"No…" said Vickers, vaguely, then returned to the present and announced, "It's gone again, I'm afraid."

"Leave it alone," I advised. "Allow it to return of its own accord, that way you'll know it truly belongs to you."

"Did the birth certificate yield any evidence of deceit?"

"It did not, I'm afraid, on the contrary — Ratcliffe Tenpenny, illegitimate or otherwise, is the legally recognised son of Terrence Tenpenny, of the last productive generation by that name. This leaves only Hadley."

"Hadley Tenpenny?"

"None other," I said. "Uncle to the redoubtable Victoria Tenpenny. Victoria — we don't call her Vicks — and Lager — the aforementioned clubmate — are rivals for the immense Tenpenny fortune. They were among those who broke down the door of the reading room onto the heartwarming tableau of two mortal enemies who had finally put their disputes behind them."

"The other two witnesses were, I take it, not Tenpennys."

"Thankfully, no, because I'm starting to lose track," I confessed. "No, there was the comically and, I suspect, deliberately incompetent maid, Miss Belsize. She heard the gunshots, several seconds apart, I remind you. And a chap named Kimberly Brickstock, likes to be called 'Burlap', for reasons best left unexplored."

"Of Brickstock and Son, sir?" asked Vickers, visibly impressed.

"Seems likely," I said. "Doubtless he has parents."

"Brickstock and Son is a City trading house of considerable consequence," said Vickers. "They are understood to dominate in areas of underwriting and large-scale bond issues."

"You don't say," I said, mirroring Vickers' admiration. "None of those small- or medium-scale bond issues for Brickstock and Son, then."

"No, sir."

"It's stepping dangerously outside of my area of expertise, I confess, but I'm going to estimate that the larger-scale the bond issue, the easier it must be. I've met Burlesque Brickstock, and were he forced in court to put two and two together, you'd have to give me odds if you wanted me to back him to get it right first try."

"The firm is a very old one, sir," clarified Vickers. "The 'Son' in question is the late Sir Meredith Brickstock, who left us in 1871."

"Well, that explains it," I said. "The current glory of Brickstock youth appears to invest whatever wit he has in trying to extort Victoria Tenpenny into matrimony. It would serve his purposes very neatly if the fortune was to go to Lager. In aid of that, Vickers, what do you know of a gentleman's club called The Swashbucklers Society?"

"It is a relatively new club, sir, established in the 1860s. It occupies the first two floors of a building in the Strand."

"What are the whispers about the members?"

"It's hardly my place, sir."

"It's exactly your place, Vickers, as my eyes and ears on the seamy underside of the gritty metropolis. Spill forth."

"Allow me to say only that no member of the Swashbucklers Society has ever been ejected for a breach of ethics." Vickers began clearing away the tea tray, which is about as close as he ever comes to actually saying out loud, 'Now, don't push it.'

"Very well," I retreated, strategically. "You know, I met a most extraordinary girl today, Vickers, working as, of all things, a parish clerk. As is so for a peculiarly large number of women that I meet, she was roundly perfect but for one terminal flaw. Later, I met her equally extraordinary grandmother, who also happened to be nanny to Ratcliffe Tenpenny."

"Tenpenny?" queried Vickers. He quickly unfolded upward from the tea tray and, in the process, spilt the sugar and caused several vertebrae to come to blows.

"That's what I said, Vickers, and I may as well warn you now, there's a greater than even chance that I'll say it again. Has the name some meaning for you, finally?"

"It does," said Vickers, endeavouring to conceal his pride in something remembered. "A Mister Tristian Tenpenny called for you today, sir."

"Lager? What did he have to say?"

Vickers stared helplessly at me for a moment, but then had a second epiphany and looked down at the pocket of his goldfinch waistcoat, the one he wears when he means to polish the silver, and then invariably forgets to polish the silver. Happily, I invest little of my self-worth in the glimmer of my silver. From the pocket he withdrew a note in his own handwriting.

"Mister Tenpenny bids you not to worry, he and Mister Proctor have deduced the meaning of the clue and the location of the tontine."

# CHAPTER NINE

# The Breakthrough Clue to the Fireproof Flue

Springtime and summer were negotiating peacefully overhead. Summer was represented by a cyan sea with a sunny disposition, and spring by a drifting continent of grey but generally agreeable cloud. After one of Vickers' not atypically eclectic breakfasts of French beans and potted salmon, I armed myself with a precautionary umbrella and walked a pleasantly metropolitan half an hour from Kensington to the hidden heart of Pimlico.

I called at number one, Wedge Hedge Square, purely for form's sake, but felt quite sure that the day's intrigue was to be played out on the main stage of number fifty-seven. Nevertheless, the door was pulled open almost immediately, as though by someone departing the moment I arrived.

"Good morning, Miss Belsize," I wished upon the startled maid. "Is Mister Tenpenny in?"

The grey and wizened head spun like an owl's to glance back into the house, and then returned with a relieved countenance, like an owl who's just got away with a misdemeanour.

"No, he's not," said Miss Belsize. She had in one hand an umbrella — a little stagey for my tastes, with a mallard-head handle — and in the other a bottle of Gordon's. "He's at the big house."

"Frankly, Miss Belsize, I'm pleased to have the opportunity to speak to you without Mister Tenpenny's awesome presence. You strike me as the timid sort, and I believe that authority dampens your willingness to speak frankly."

"Timid? Me?"

"You hide it well."

"I don't hide nothing," said Miss Belsize, folding her arms in such a fashion as to entirely obscure the umbrella and bottle of gin.

"Let us say, then, that you are a woman of discretion," I conceded. "Tell me something, Miss Belsize, I realise that you have many competing demands on your time and attention, but do you recall the duel?"

"Of course I remember the duel."

"Excellent," I said, for I know the value of judicious praise. "You mentioned that you first heard the shots from the back garden of number three, and that there were two of them, several seconds apart."

"That's right."

"You're quite sure about that."

"Course I am."

"And you're equally certain about where you were at the time."

Miss Belsize didn't answer this, unless a knuckled brow and derisive snort count as a reply and I believe that, to Miss Belsize, they did.

"I mean, behind the house," I continued, "So, with number three and most of number fifty-seven between you and the closing ceremony, you still managed to clearly make out two, distinct shots."

"Nothing unusual about that," commented the maid casually. "Gunshots is very loud."

"My point exactly, Miss Belsize."


Back on the sidewalk, waiting to escort me safely to my next destination, was Old Nick on four legs, his head cocked to the side with a distinct 'is it your impression that you are my only responsibility today?' In that instant, however, his ear-and-a-half swivelled in the direction of the entrance to the square and in the next instant the dog was a blur of yipping and clattering on an interception trajectory with a bowler-capped coroner.

Babbage affected to take no notice of the dog, but nevertheless occasionally succumbed to the temptation to swat about with his soft briefcase. Neither inspiringly athletic nor frenetically energetic, the efforts were largely symbolic and would have appeared to the uninformed observer more as a man expressing an irreconcilable grievance with his soft briefcase.

"Hullo, Mister Babbage," I hailed as he approached. "Lovely morning."

I'd caught the coroner mid-flail and he required a moment to compose himself.

"Mister, ah…"

"Boisjoly," I helpfully supplied. "Of the Kensington, tram-bothering branch."

"Oh, yes. Of course. Good morning." There was something grudging about the salutation, but I put it down to lingering resentment for the added paperwork through which my father put the poor man.

"I confess, I'm surprised — pleasantly, of course — but surprised nevertheless to see you back at Wedge Hedge Square," I said. "I had received the impression that you felt there was nothing more to be done."

I fell in next to Babbage as he continued along the sidewalk toward number fifty-seven, and Lucifer fell in next to me.

"There *is* nothing more to be done," grumbled Babbage, but trudged on all the same. "That Wittersham chap tells me that there's documentary evidence to that effect in the possession of some half-wit." Some thought struck Babbage at this point, and he ceased his rapid stalking and drew himself up. "Did he mean you?"

"Might have," I confessed. "Did he say merely 'half-wit'? Or 'meddlesome half-wit'? That'll be the clincher."

"No, just half-wit."

"Well, it remains a broad field, Mister Babbage, but I expect the inspector means Chauncy Proctor, Tenpenny family solicitor, and the document in question is a contract between the deceased parties, agreeing to settle their differences by way of a duel."

"Those two cretins entered into a contract to shoot each other?" Babbage continued his march and I continued alongside, much to the satisfaction of Lucifer, who I felt was beginning to look upon me as sort of deputy. "Is Proctor sorting out that tontine business then?"

"I fear not," I said. "Is it relevant to the inquest?"

"If you'll be so good as to search your memory, Mister

Boisjoly, you'll recall that I've already said there is no call for an inquest. I realise that much ground has been covered since then, but perhaps if you were to take notes, or make up some little mnemonic..."

"Perhaps you are unaware that the maid heard two shots, seconds apart," I suggested. "You yourself said that both men died instantly, leading one to the inevitable conclusion that there was a third party."

"Or an echo."

"Is that likely?" I asked.

"I don't know. Why ask me?"

"Isn't that precisely the sort of question that gets settled by an inquest?"

"You want to be coroner?"

"Most manifestly not, no," I answered with a reflexive and yet heartfelt certitude.

"Back in '26, you could have been, you know." We had reached the entrance to number fifty-seven now and Babbage stopped before the steps to ruminate on a golden past. "The only qualification was you had to own property in the county. It's how I ended up yoked to it — inherited the lot from my father, curse him."

"Far be it from me to propose depriving the city of a dedicated professional, Mister Babbage, but why don't you simply retire from the field?" I asked. "I expect there are any number of alternative disciplines that would benefit from a man of your explosive energy. Still life model, comes immediately to mind."

"I do solemnly, sincerely and truly declare, Boisjoly, I've met mangled corpses with better retention than you have," declared Babbage solemnly, sincerely, etc. "I've just told you — they changed the law. Now any new county coroner has to be 'qualified' — a barrister or medical doctor or some such fiddly nonsense. Prior to '26, I could have just sold the property and the job and gone to Yeovil to grow Mangel-Wurzels, whatever they are. Now all I've got is the property, and little chance of selling that, now Tenpenny's escaped his commitments."

"This sounds intriguing, Mister Babbage," I said. "To which Tenpenny do you refer and, I may as well tack on the follow-up question, to which commitment?"

"Both of them. Either of them. Doesn't much matter now, does it?" said Babbage. "The family always wanted my bit of land, just behind this house..." Babbage frowned in gesture toward number fifty-seven, "...with a view to making Wedge Hedge Square give onto Belgrave Road."

Before I could pursue this curious line, the door to number fifty-seven burst open and Lager called "Anty!" with a wild, new year's eve tone. Then, spotting Babbage, he melted back to his normal, sedate humour, and said, "...and Mister Babbage. How pleasant."

"There a half-wit here called Proctor?" asked Babbage.

"Proctor... Proctor..." repeated Lager, while appearing to muse on a passing cloud.

"He means Chancy, Lager," I clarified. "He's here for the contract."

"Oh, Chancy. And the contract. Yes, yes they're both here, Mister Babbage. Do come in."

"And I'm here because of the peculiar message you left with my man," I said, as we negotiated the doorway.

"Message? What message?"

"You told him that you'd sorted out the clue, and had

found the tontine."

"What? No. Ha. Ah, ha. Ha. No. No tontine. No." Lager continued this sustained sputter as he bade us into the salon. "He must have got it wrong. Didn't you tell me your man was about a hundred and two years old? I only told him that Chancy still hadn't found the clue and, ehm, and that we weren't too much bothered about it. That's all."

"You came round to Kensington to tell me that?"

"To your man, yes."

Chancy was there, just as he'd been two days prior, but instead of sitting on the divan, smiling vacantly and holding a whisky-and-soda, he was sitting on the divan, smiling vacantly and holding a cup of tea.

"Tea, Anty? Mister Babbage?" Lager busied himself with the tea things with the maladroit enthusiasm of an infant with a jangly set of keys. "Chancy, this is Mister Babbage, county coroner. Mister Babbage has come for the contract. That's right, isn't it, Mister Babbage?"

"I have no idea why I'm here," said Babbage, inflicting his weight on an ill-prepared wing chair. "Sweet and white, if you please."

Lager splashed random ratios of tea, milk and sugar into a cup and handed it over.

"Contract, Chancy," Lager urged the solicitor, who appeared to have been daydreaming.

"Oh, right-ho," said Chancy. He pulled the document from his breast pocket and handed it to the coroner, who opened and, by all appearances, applied to it the very latest in speed-reading techniques. He slipped the contract into his briefcase and leaned back with his tea.

"More tea, Mister Babbage?" asked Lager solicitously.

"I haven't touched this one yet."

"Quite right. Anty?"

"Still waiting for mine, old kidney," I pointed out. It was never to be, though, because in that moment Vicks and her persistent fiancé, Kimberly Brickstock, appeared at the door of the salon.

"Morning Victoria, Barley," I said. "You're just in time for tea."

"We're not here for tea," declared Vicks, but it was too late to stop Brickstock, who was already pulling an ottoman up to the tea trolley.

"No buns?" he said.

"Chauncy Proctor," I said, stepping in where I knew Lager would forget to go, "may I present Kimberly Brickstock, of Brickstock and Son. Likes to be called Barfly."

"Burly," corrected Barfly.

"Burpy."

"Burly."

"And this is Mister Babbage," I said, for I was running out of variations. "Mister Babbage is the county coroner."

"Oh, yes?" said Brickstock. "I've a thing or two to tell you about what happened here the other day."

Babbage held up a 'stop right there' left hand while deftly sipping his tea with his right, and then said, "The office of the county coroner no longer has any interest in the affair."

"You haven't even heard what I have to say," pouted Brickstock.

"A status quo which I mean to assiduously preserve," said Babbage. He balanced his saucer on the arm of the chair and took to his feet.

"But this bloke told me the inspector from Scotland Yard was waiting to hear my views," complained Brickstock, gesturing at me with a half a Garibaldi. "And when I got here he was gone."

"The inspector isn't one to let the grass grow," I explained. "And you know how you will linger over your sticky buns, Biro old man."

"You should hear me out, Mister Babbage," Brickstock assured the coroner.

"I shall add it to the bottom of a long, long list of life's regrets, Mister Brickstock." Babbage put his hat on his head, hammered it home with the palm of his hand, said, "Good day," and gambolled out the door. In a moment, the sound of the front door opening and then closing was heard.

Lager skidded into the hall to watch after the coroner.

"He's gone."

"Is he coming back?" asked Brickstock.

"Not in the near term," I answered.

"Are the police coming back?"

"Why don't you tell me what it is that you wish to share with the inspector, Boilerplate?" I proposed. "He and I are as one mind on most issues unrelated to haberdashery and amateur detection."

"No offence, Boisjoly," said Brickstock, as one does when one is about to give offence. "I doubt very much you'd follow my line of reasoning. There's a meeting of minds among professional men that the idle class can't be expected to understand."

"Oh, I don't know," I said in my defence. "My own club — no idler a bunch known to man — is home to one of the nation's more renowned mixology research foundations, consulted by industry and government alike. I take it you've heard and possibly partaken of *The Sloe Train To Sunrise?* That was us."

Brickstock considered this defence of my people through the prism of glowering eyebrows, blinked it away, and pursued another theme, "Tell you one thing I'm going to take up with Scotland Yard, though, that thieving maid, Battersea."

"Belsize, I think you mean."

"That's it — Belsize. She nicked my umbrella when I was here last."

"Then your plan is the only way forward, Bunting," I assured him. "I know that Inspector Wittersham takes a very dim view of the pilfering of umbrellas and walking sticks. Indeed, only last month he presented a tract to the Law Society proposing special judicial status for the British whangee."

"You needn't get the police involved, Burly old chap," chided Lager. "Anything for which Miss Belsize has yet to find a market is easily retrieved from below stairs."

"Can we get on with it?" exasperated Vicks. "Why did you ask Miss Belsize to tell me that you needed me here this morning?"

"Because he's determined the location of the tontine and he wants you on hand when it's revealed," I said.

Lager's smug smile sagged to a curious comma.

"How the devil did you know that?" he asked.

"You told me yourself," I said. "Barring a breakfast of absinthe and orange juice, it was the only interpretation I could charitably put on that under-rehearsed pantomime you performed for Mister Babbage."

"You don't suppose he twigged, do you?" Lager looked reflexively toward the door. "He'd just take it away as evidence."

"No way of knowing," I adjudged. "The twigged Babbage and the untwigged Babbage are functionally identical — he couldn't possibly manage to care less."

"What's this about finding the tontine?" asked Vicks. "I thought the Proctor family braintrust had it."

"Oh, no," corrected Chancy, with the tone of one expressing pride in a job well done, "Terrence Tenpenny took it away from us years ago."

"And left in its place a cryptic clue," continued Lager. "But Chancy and I have figured it out. You'll never guess where it is."

"In the reading room?" guessed Vicks.

"No, it's… actually that's right. How did you know?"

"Where else would you think I'd never guess?" answered Vicks with the dying embers of her patience. "Let's have a look at it then."

"Right." Lager put down his teacup and saucer and clapped his hands together. "Chancy, if you please."

Chancy stood and withdrew a slip of paper from his vest pocket, and then took a little bow. He held up the paper and opened his mouth to speak the words he saw there when Vicks said "Can we just get on with it?"

"Actually, Vicks, we haven't recovered the deed itself, as such," explained Lager. "We wanted there to be witnesses. Chancy's idea."

"Oh, well, if it's on the advice of the worst solicitor in

London, no wonder you insisted on it."

"What does it say, Chancy?" I asked.

Chancy cleared his throat and, I fancy, would have liked to run through a couple of voice exercises, but then leapt right to his big scene, "The first clue is… a crown, indicated by the keystone of the second archway in the hall."

"What's a keystone?" asked Vicks.

"It's part of an arch," explained Lager, who had done an Italian Renaissance Architecture optional in his final year to get out of that season's fox hunt, owing to an embarrassing incident the previous autumn involving a neighbouring Pomeranian which, to be fair, do rather resemble foxes.

"Fine," sighed Vicks. "What's the second clue?"

"There is no second clue, Vicks, it's a sort of scavenger hunt. The first clue leads to the second clue." As he said this, Lager herded us into the hall. There, he stood beneath the second archway, his arms outstretched, as though about to bestow benediction.

"Et… *voilà.*" He stepped one move to the right, like a rook, revealing the tile on which he stood. The *trompe l'oeil,* three-dimensional effect was herein considerably undermined by the wrong tile altogether — what should have been a black triangle on a white tile (or a white pentagon on a black tile, according to taste) was a white square decorated with a crown, like the royal head-gear on a chess piece.

"Is that the queen from the floor of the reading room?" I asked.

"Well spotted, Anty," said Lager. "It is. And that, obviously, is the next clue, if you'll all follow me…" Lager spun on his heel and led us triumphantly toward the reading room.

We single-filed down the hall like floats in a parade in honour of the human condition. Brickstock followed Lager, pridefully marching with his hands behind his back and baffled concentration on his front. Vicks wandered behind him with her eyes cast heavenward in despair for the folly of man and men. Next was Chancy, innocently taking in the scenery and appearing to be very much at risk of getting lost in a straight hallway. I brought up the rear representing, at least on a comparative basis, wisdom.

The reading room was largely as last seen, with the notable exception that nobody in it was dead. The place seemed sunnier and more spacious without murder victims, and on balance I think I preferred it that way — it had that *je ne sais quoi* of a room without dead bodies in it.

"Well?" posed Lager. He had positioned himself facing us, his back to the windows and the fireplace to his left.

"I admit, that is pretty convincing," said Vicks, looking at the floor.

"Yes, yes, quite conclusive," concurred Brickstock, with his hand on his chin and his eyes on the windows, having clearly missed the point, which was the tiles. The chess motif charted out on the floor of the reading room was mostly complete and formed of black and white tiles with symbols — ramparts, horses' heads, bishops' hats, crowns, etc. — imposed on them in the opposite colour. From where Lager stood, he was playing black, but the pieces were in the wrong order, and the king and queen were missing altogether.

The white pieces were correctly positioned — rook, knight, bishop, queen, king, bishop, knight, rook. Facing them, however, reading from left to right, was rook, knight, bishop, bishop, knight, rook, tile missing from the hall.

What's more, the tile was positioned such that it formed with the tile next to it an arrow, and they pointed directly into the fireplace, which protruded to where the rook tile would have been.

"It's behind the fireplace," declared Lager.

The fireplace, as mentioned previously, was an electric contraption installed in front of the older enamel back panel. It was this enamel back panel which Lager now menaced with chisel and hammer, which he had prepared and left on the writing desk with malice aforethought.

"Do we really think it likely that Terrence Tenpenny, so soon after having rescued the tontine from Chancy's grandfather, would entrust such valuable papers to a fireplace?" I asked no one in particular.

"I expect that's just what he was presuming people would think," concluded Lager. "Doubtless there'll be an asbestos lining or something."

A broker's son, a solicitor, a Juniper and two Tenpennys took up hammer and chisel and considered the job at hand. Lager performed the actual vandalism, aided by the dubious but generous advice and criticism of the spectator class, and together we quickly made a right hash of the job. The trick with breaking through enamel tile, we all assumed, was to chip carefully away at the grouting until individual tiles could be removed. That may remain a truism of the trade, but it requires more finesse than Lager was prepared to bring to the task, and from a standing start he went from 'gently chipping' to 'brutally smashing' in what would certainly be record time if records were kept for that sort of thing.

The principal issue, it seems, is that the grouting was very old, and had over time become as much a part of the enamel tile as the enamel. Lager would tap away in a vertical line and from the spot would spring two diagonal cracks and one horizontal. Finally, Lager did what he might just as well have done from the start — he stood, hefted the hammer over his shoulder as though laying up a game-changing backhand, and gave the crackling mess a whack it would remember for all its days. The effect was pleasing. Lager flashed us all a satisfied smile and then proceeded to indiscriminately smash away the remnants of the old tile.

The interior, which was in the form of a brick vault, was indeed lined with asbestos. It was a very safe, inconspicuous cavern in which to hide a document, which no one would ever find.

"It's gone," said Lager, putting into words that which we all observed as we looked into the dark, empty space.

# CHAPTER TEN

# The Salacious Stories of the Swashbucklers Society

Where the Strand becomes Fleet Street, the literal border of literacy and journalism, in one of those impossibly narrow, 17th century English Baroque, granite wedding cakes, I found the small but distinguished chambers of the Swashbucklers Society.

It was a modest little club, with just a discreet brass plaque outside and, in the foyer, no porter. Instead, there was a taxidermied adult Bengal tiger, rampant, like the coat of arms of the Bombay regiment, except this one was wearing a bowler hat and carrying about a dozen umbrellas.

The rest of the foyer was essentially staging for the tiger in a hat — deep, rosewood panelled walls, Persian carpets flowing up low, marble stairs with brass bannisters, and a copper and crystal chandelier in the form of an airship.

"Ahh!" From behind me, coming through the door, was the unmistakable call of the colonial class, about to make a point. The tone is often accompanied by the jingling of medals and always followed by helpful advice regarding how a chap my age might better profit from his time. "Admiring old Roscoe, are you?"

In fact, the imperial poobah was constructed in line with the growing trend toward miniaturisation; short, slight, light and wiry, with a neatly clipped leading-man moustache and silver hair combed hard against his scalp in a manner suggestive of a punitive measure. He looked rather like Douglas Fairbanks, reduced for forty-five minutes on a low heat. He hung his umbrella on the tiger's aggressive left arm and said, "Had him stuffed just as he was when I shot him, don't you know."

"Surely not wearing that bowler," I surmised.

"No, not wearing that bowler," said the poobah, gazing meditatively at Roscoe the tiger. "Most uncanny thing, though, he was wearing a Homburg. Point of fact, that hat saved my life. I was playing whist with the Maharaja of Bharatpur — a hundred rupees a point — and as was tradition at the time when he owed me over a thousand rupees — about two hundred pounds measured in good English ale — the Maharaja pulled a revolver from his robes with the intention of cancelling the debt. Same moment, Roscoe here wanders in off the terrace. I doubt old Brijindar would have been so nonplussed had the beast not been wearing a brand new Homburg — Lord knows where he got it or how he kept it on his head — but the Maharaja lets out a yell and starts shooting wildly. Roscoe, of course, assumes the attitude in which you see him now, I relieve the maharaja of the pistol and plug the poor beast. Caius Potts."

"Eh?"

"I'm Caius Potts," clarified the poobah, and held out his hand to illustrate the point.

"Anthony Boisjoly," I reciprocated. "Are you a member of the Swashbucklers, Mister Potts?"

"Among one of the oldest and most reprobate, either of

which is saying a great deal."

"Is there a committee, or member thereof, with whom I could speak?" I asked.

"Not thinking of joining, are you, young man?" Caius Potts took a step back and appraised the Boisjoly candidacy. "The membership committee is rather an ad hoc sort of affair, if you will, due to the absence of space." Potts gestured toward the deep, cluttered tunnel that was the interior of the club. "No room for new members until a current member leaves us."

"I'm afraid that's just what I've come to report, Mister Potts — do you know a Swashbuckler called Hadley Tenpenny?"

"Finally got him, did they?" Potts nodded knowingly. "How did he go?"

"Duel," I said. "Shot through the heart."

"I say, what an extraordinary turnabout." Potts relieved me of my umbrella and put it in the care of Roscoe. "Best come along in, then, and meet the membership committee."

The Swashbucklers interior aesthetic was not unlike that of Hadley's floor at Wedge Hedge Square, though with something more of a blood-letting theme curated in animal-head trophies, stuffed wildcats, and an extensive weapons cache. The main floor had only enough space, in fact, for the mementoes of glorious slaughter and a narrow staircase to the first floor, where the action was playing out in the form of chattering clubmen all about Hadley's age and general countenance, engaging in what appeared to be animated discussion of animated things. The salon was otherwise much like that of any other gentlemen's club, apart from the spears and masks and general buccaneering spirit. The steward wore a fez.

"Gin Kala Khatta, for me," said Potts to the man in the fez as we positioned ourselves on worked leather odeon chairs by the front window, overlooking Fleet Street. "What's your poison, Boisjoly?"

"Oh, same, obviously," I said. "Haven't had a decent gin and whatever you just said in donkey's."

"Same for my guest, Tharrawaddy," Potts added to the order. "And ask Mister Crocker if he can spare us a moment."

Tharrawaddy, who had the very distinct appearance of someone who, when he wasn't wearing a fez, was a much happier person named Bob, wheeled away and spoke briefly to a beefy, jowly chap with a handlebar moustache and eyebrows that, together, could have been sheared to weave a substantial rug. The steward interrupted him as he was acting out what appeared from that distance to have been a foxtrot fought in opposition to someone doing a waltz.

"Hello, you old card cheat," said the jowly man I took to be Crocker. "What's all this then?"

Crocker found his own odeon chair and cocked a curious eyebrow like the mane of a pantomime horse.

"Anthony Boisjoly... Dial Crocker," said Potts by way of breaking down the barriers. "Mister Boisjoly tells me that old Tenpenny has finally cashed in his chips, and that he wishes to be considered for the consequent vacancy."

In point of fact, I had no interest in joining the Swashbucklers Society nor in giving the impression that I had, but in that instant I realised the potential benefit in presenting as at least a prospective insider. Gentlemens' clubs are often accused, with some justification, I think, of being somewhat clubby.

"Snakebite," declared Crocker, in a definitive tone.

"No, actually, shot through the heart in a duel," I said.

"Eh?" Crocker, it turned out, had been speaking to Tharrawaddy, who had returned with our drinks. "Snakebite for me, double lao kao." That business done, he returned his attention to the passing of Hadley Tenpenny. "Duel, eh? Rather darkly ironic, eh, what, Potts? Jealous husband, I suppose."

"His distant cousin, Ratcliffe Tenpenny," I said. "It was something in the order of settling an outstanding financial dispute." I left that in the air for the moment while I tasted my first Gin Kala Khatta, which was a tall, inky, icy concoction that tasted rather like what having my ear twisted would taste like if it were a drink. "Might I ask why you assume that, if Hadley Tenpenny were to expire in a duel, it would be at the hand of a jealous husband?"

Crocker and Potts shared a cheeky glance.

"Amazing he lived this long," adjudged Potts.

"Remember the bother he got himself into in South Africa?" asked Crocker, to which I, of course, responded in the negative — I did not recall the bother in South Africa.

"Ran into him purely by chance at an underground casino in Maasvlakte," obliged Potts. "He was deliberately losing at Morabaraba, if memory serves. He was with a group of missionaries who knew him by the name of Von Balmoos, so he greeted me in Swahili and told me to play along. Turns out he'd gotten himself married to the daughter of a tribal chief up in the Zambezi Valley, which was problematic enough, but he already had some sort of questionable arrangement with the daughter of the Italian trade attaché in Johannesburg. He gave me his eyepatch and I gave him my berth on the SS *Falstaff* bound for Suriname, and I spent a very agreeable winter as the choirmaster of Saint Thomas in the Glen in Maseru. Thank you, Tharrawaddy."

Crocker received his drink — a thick, grass-green ooze in a champagne *coupe* — before continuing his story; "It was only when I was negotiating passage on a tramp steamer to Mutsamudu, in the Comoros you understand, that the chickens came home to roost. I was still operating under the name Von Balmoos — I'd traded my Maltese passport for some ostrich biltong — when I was tracked down by two Sicilians with a message from the Italian trade attaché — I'd marry his daughter, and be well quick about it, or get used to life without working legs."

"Stout fellow." Potts raised his beaker of pinchy ink in recognition of the Swashbuckler spirit.

"Least I could do," Crocker waved away the praise, "after Hadley ransomed me in Kabul."

"He was dashed fond of that goat, too," mused Potts.

"Your legs appear to be largely operational now, Mister Crocker," I observed.

Crocker faced off against his drink, raised it with one hand while pinching his nose with the other, and then swallowed it in a single throw, before replying, "Well, they were Sicilian assassins, weren't they? Easily bought off, I mean to say. I traded my continued good health for the location of a fortune in diamonds buried on the banks of Lake Victoria, Uganda shore. Wild goose chase, of course — I gave them elaborate and precise directions that would, if followed very carefully, lead to the geographic centre of the Congo Basin in time for the rainy season."

"You don't happen to know if any issue resulted from Hadley's entanglements in South Africa, do you?" I asked, about as diplomatically as that sort of thing can be asked.

"Not to my certain knowledge," said Potts, vaguely.

"Nor mine," agreed Crocker. "Stands to reason, though. If not South Africa then certainly Darjeeling or that business in the Aegean Sea."

"Or Rupert's Land."

"Or Montevideo."

"Oh, yes, indeed, Montevideo," Potts recalled, somehow simultaneously scandalised and amused.

"I can't help noticing a theme developing here," I observed. "And I'm quite curious to examine it with respect to something both of you have mentioned in your turn — why is it particularly ironic that Hadley Tenpenny died in a duel?"

Americans, in that colourful way they have of making everything about poker or baseball, might say that I had overplayed my hand while the bases were fully loaded, or some such thing. Crocker and Potts shared a meaningful glance, and then turned the spotlight on me.

"You know, Mister Boisjoly," Potts levelled at me, "the Swashbucklers Society isn't for the, shall we say, curious." There was something about the rhythm of 'shall we say' that strongly suggested that it was a delaying tactic, while he constructed a diplomatic alternative to 'shall we say, nosy'.

"Indeed not," agreed Crocker. "Members are expected to contribute to the lore and glory of the society."

"Of course. I would have expected nothing less," I credibly claimed. "Mind you, I'm still young."

"Time I was your age I'd been tried for insurrection in the Dutch West Indies," said Crocker.

"And I'd nearly died of curare poisoning in the Amazon Basin," countered Potts.

Among my kin and kind I'm regarded as quite well-travelled, but the principal and persistent theme to my choice of destination and accommodation has always been luxury. The more the better, in my view, and if it runs to a few bob extra for a view of the basilica, so be it. Doubtless standing trial for a capital crime and curare poisoning have their charms, along with swimming in shark-infested waters and skiing *hors-piste* at night, but first-class travel to five-star hotels rarely if ever offers such glamorous opportunity.

I think the greatest hardship I've ever endured in my travels was aboard Lord and Lady Hannibal-Pool's yacht in the summer of '24 when, owing to a tragic language mixup in Porto Cristo, we boarded two crates of caviar and literally not a crumb of bread. The poor chef did his sturdy best but when, by Sunday morning, we'd resorted to spreading the stuff on fried eggs, feelings were running high. We had to change course for Monaco and take on a consignment of *socca* and it's probably no exaggeration to say that lives were spared.

"I don't suppose it compares to the opportunities for adventure offered by Britain's bold, buccaneering past," I began, "but there was that time I was shanghaied aboard Captain Hannibal-Pool's schooner when he smuggled a thousand cases of Sicilian grappa into Portsmouth under cover of darkness." This was based partially in reality. I wasn't so much shanghaied, though, as required to join the voyage at Valencia by my mother, who hoped that I might hit it off with the Hannibal-Pools' daughter, whose first name escapes me — I can only recall now the affectionate sobriquet I'd developed for her by the end of the first day at sea, 'Whinging Cow'. Winnifred, possibly. The part about grappa was entirely true.

"Forced to sleep in a rum barrel, I was." This was something of an exaggeration, but I did have a starboard-side stateroom without its own bar facilities. "When I could sleep, that is — I was effectively a slave aboard that ship." Lady Hannibal-Pool assigns duties to all her guests — I was in charge of ice. "Nothing to eat at all but Sturgeon roe, black as tar and salty as the sea itself, such that no amount of champagne could offset."

"Champagne?" queried Potts. "You had champagne?"

"Champagne?" I lobbed back. "No, of course not."

"You said champagne."

"I was in shackles, sir, from sunup to sundown." I rapidly corrected course. "I was in chain pain. It's a common nautical term."

"I see."

"Finally, we put into some hidden cove for supplies," I continued, recalling the natural deepwater port of Monaco. "I went ashore as part of a foraging party. Once there, I stole away from my captors and, with a gold filling that I removed with a fish hook, bought into a game of pinfinger with a privateer who went by the name of Eight-Finger Louis. He was experienced with the knife, but I had the advantage of all five fingers on my left hand." It was not, in fact, Pinfinger, but Baccarat that I played that night in Monte Carlo, and in the original version the role of Eight-Finger Louis was played by His Highness Prince Louis II. And I lost my shirt.

"By morning," I said, for the sun was indeed rising over the dome of the *Café de Paris* as we stumbled out of the *Casino de Monte Carlo*, "I'd won enough to purchase passage on a whaler bound for Algiers." This, too, had a grain of truth to it, but instead of a whaler and Algiers, it was the Royce-Phipps' steam yacht and Antibes.

"I say," said Potts, visibly moved by my tale. "What became of this Hannibal-Pool fellow?"

"We keep in touch."

"You keep in touch?"

"Put him up for membership of the Juniper."

"Your club?"

"One doesn't like to hold a grudge," I said casually, "and in light of his daughter's wedding earlier this year I can only assume that he was forced to sell his boat to pay the dowry, poor chap."

I sipped my Gin Kala Khatta because, in the interval, I'd forgotten that it tasted like a vinegar derived from turnips. Nevertheless, it gave my hosts an opportunity to voicelessly communicate some verdict in that eyebrow semaphore known only to gentlemen who went to school together sometime prior to the Crimean War.

"Always avoid Algiers myself," commented Crocker. "Got stabbed there once by a Macaque."

"What was it that you were asking about poor Hadley?" asked Potts.

"I suppose, simply put, is it so that this last duel wasn't his first?"

"It is," confirmed Potts. "You tell it, Dial."

"Quite right," agreed Crocker. "It started when Hadley and I went to Damascus to settle a bet. Poor blighter thought he could handle a camel better than I — I let him talk, of course, but I was breaking dromedaries in Al Qassim when he was still learning to ride elephants on the Malabar. We lost track of each other during all that business with Muhanna Salih Abaalkhail. There's a chap who knows what he wants, I can tell you — had to walk all the way to Medina disguised as a Hijazi spice merchant just to avoid becoming his minister of defence."

"And Hadley?"

"Treasury secretary, I believe. I went south, he went north. Made it as far as Tripoli, where he fell in with some Frenchmen who were getting up an expedition to capture a live Scylla."

"But not Charybdis?" I asked. "The way Homer tells it in *The Odyssey*, the Scylla and Charybdis were something of a matching set."

"Apparently the skipper had some sort of standing complaint against the Scylla, and was indifferent to the Charybdis," explained Crocker. "In any case, Hadley crewed with them as far as Mykonos, where he joined an English yachting party of his acquaintance."

"You don't happen to recall the names of the yachting party, do you?" I asked. "A story is so much more relatable with a cast list, don't you find?"

"Never mentioned, for reasons which will become obvious," said Crocker.

"Ah. Of course. One doesn't bandy a lady's name."

"What makes you say that a woman was involved?" asked Potts, fixing me with the jaundiced eye of the senior vote of a membership committee.

"Isn't there always?" I philosophised. *"Cherchez la femme."*

"Well, indeed, there *was* a woman involved," conceded Crocker. "Hadley, however, was never very averse to the practice of bandying a lady's name. Made something of a point of it, if the truth be known."

"Then what was the source of his uncharacteristic reticence on this occasion?" I asked.

"Why, the duel." Crocker said this as though he was pointing out the nose on my face. "Isn't that what you were asking about?"

"The duel over the unbandied party," I surmised.

"Correct," confirmed Crocker. "Fought with skeet-shooting rifles, of all things, on a yacht."

"Unorthodox, I'll grant you," I granted, "but hardly off the beaten track by the exacting standards of the Swashbucklers Society."

"I believe the peculiarity was the manner in which Hadley emerged victorious," commented Potts. "Swashbucklers, above all, survive."

"And how did Hadley survive in this case?" I asked, for form's sake, for I had already worked out the answer.

"Bit of money exchanged below decks, some sleight of hand in the gun room," said Crocker, casually, "and his opponent's weapon was loaded with blank ammunition."

# CHAPTER ELEVEN

# Alleged from the Edge of a Wedge Hedge Ledge

If they ever strike the right chemical balance and manage to bottle that specific combination of springtime, blossoms, breeze, horses, and tar, it will be called, simply, *'London'*. Until that blessed day, however, the only place to find it is in the wild and in the moment, and the morning after my interview for entry to the Swashbucklers Society, Wedge Hedge Square had it in buckets.

The fenced garden appeared to have cast aside all reservations and wrapped itself in its brightest seasonal fashion. Pink and white honeysuckle blooms peeked with unguarded anticipation through the bars. The delightfully unkempt grasses hushed and swooned with the light wind. The hulking elms displayed a full consignment of all the essentials — bugs, buds, birds, and the like — and, less typically, one dubious solicitor.

"Hullo, Chancy," I called up to the broad, accommodating branch on which he sat. "Lovely day for it, at least."

"Hello, Anty." Chancy smiled and ventured a slight wave that nearly cost him his balance. "I'm up a tree."

"I see that, Chancy old man, and I applaud it, thoroughly. We would all of us do well to remember that the boyish joy of grand adventure to be found in streams and up trees doesn't abandon us, it is we who push it away."

"I was chased here by that rabid dog."

"Young Asmodeus, you mean?" I asked. "He's the sanest of us all, Chancy. You probably veered from the prescribed path. He has a very firm policy with regards to points A and B, and the avenues in between."

"I was just lingering."

"Ah, well, there you go," I said. "The dog has many duties to which to attend, and cannot tolerate loitering. Are you coming down, at some point? I would share with you some developments."

"Can you give me a hand?"

"I can but try, Chancy, but it's my experience — hard-won, I should add — that getting down from trees is largely a one-man job."

"I used that bench to climb up," Chancy looked down at, presumably, the aforementioned bench, obscured by the foliage, "but I kicked it over in the effort. Could you upright it?"

"That I can do, with almost no further direction."

I found the gate and was instantly lost. The grass and weeds and saplings were so thoroughly in the *laissez-faire* tradition of the English garden that, had it not been for Chancy functioning as a beacon, I'd have been forced to return to base camp.

"There you are, old man," I said, righting a rustic wooden bench beneath Chancy's branch.

"Ta, very." Chancy slipped gingerly and, dare I say it,

expertly, the two or three inches that remained between his feet and the bench. Then he stepped to the ground and sat down for a well-deserved breather. "What brings you by? Have you figured out what happened to the tontine?"

"Yes."

Judging by his swivel-eyed reaction, this was not the answer Chancy expected.

"Not really."

"Oh, yes. I spotted the solution straight away," I assured him. "Why? You didn't continue looking for it, did you?"

"Only for a bit," said Chancy, somewhat sullenly. "Two or three hours, perhaps."

"All of you?"

"No, just Lager and I. That chap Brickstock went off to lay hands on his umbrella and Vicks left just after you did, saying she had better things to do, chief of which was not being in our company."

"You don't know if Mister Brickstock was on his way to Scotland Yard, by any chance?" I asked.

"Possibly, but he was still here when we finally gave up the search."

"But he didn't say where he was going."

"I didn't actually speak to him," said Chancy. "I was hiding behind the door of Lager's place, and he was there, on the street, between here number one. There was no escape."

"I see. Purely to pass the time, Chancy, why were you hiding from Brickstock? Did you have a sticky bun?"

"He was arguing with some woman, with considerable animation," said Chancy. "I find situations of that nature tremendously awkward."

"Was Vicks finally releasing him to pursue other opportunities?"

"I don't know who it was, and I couldn't make out what they were saying." Chancy put a hand to his chin and appeared to focus on the past. "They weren't shouting, you understand, just speaking in that hushed, insistent way people do when they're disagreeing about something about which both parties hold strong views."

"I'm familiar with it," I said, nodding. "Until I was ten years old I thought it was a language native to the land from which my parents had come."

"Anty?" Lager's familiar off-pitch baritone called out from beyond the field of flowing grasses. "Chancy? What are you doing in the garden?"

"Recapturing the peril and enterprise of childhood," I answered. "Although it's Chancy who's actually swinging through the trees. I'm mainly functioning in an advisory capacity."

"Not any mail in there, is there?" asked Lager.

I looked about us. "Not that I can see. Was the garden expecting an important letter?"

"Just pursuing a hunch," explained Lager. "The postman chucked all our mail over the fence yesterday before legging it. Closest he'd come to actually making a delivery in six months. Are you coming out?"

"Is that hound still out there?" asked Chancy with a sort of wounded disdain.

"Lucifer, you mean?" answered Lager. "No sign of him."

"Then I shall come out." Chancy raised his chin and led bravely into the jungle, back to freedom and civilisation. At the gate, he surveyed the square at length before saying, "Anty's figured out what happened to the tontine."

"Of course you did. Good show, Anty," said Lager. "Where is it?"

"Where it always was — at number fifty-seven."

"I'll see you there," said Chancy, and off he went at a dignified but prudent pace.

"Any luck re-igniting the interest of the police, Anty?" asked Lager, as we watched Chancy scurry, stop, and scurry along the path to number fifty-seven.

"I've been occupied with other avenues of enquiry," I said, "but Brickstock sounded as though he was going to take a crack at Inspector Wittersham, and he may be able to bring some old-money influence to bear. In the meantime, we can at least determine what's at stake — for all we know Chancy's forefathers traded the whole thing for a handful of magic beans generations ago."

"Poor chap." We watched Chancy struggle with the front door before realising that it opened inward. "You couldn't say looking at him, but he's got a first from Cambridge."

"You're not saying that Chauncy the Chancy Lawyer has a law degree from Cambridge," I said. "The university, let us be clear, and not, say, the train station."

"Law? No, of course not — architectural engineering and philosophy," said Lager. "You should hear him recite *Praktikê* — all Greek to me, of course, but I swear it brought a tear to my eye."

"Then what drew him to the family law practice? It's clearly neither affection nor aptitude."

"Exactly that," said Lager. "Family. When his father

botched his final brief a few years earlier than expected, Chancy felt duty-bound to step in and maintain the appallingly low standard of advice and care the firm had been offering its clients for generations."

"Yes, I can see that. It's unlikely anyone else could manage."

"I daresay not," agreed Lager. "Yesterday, after about two hours of quite thorough searching, he forgot what it was that we were looking for. I can tell you with great certainty, by the way, it's not in the reading room."

"I know. It never was."

"I suppose that's a relief to know," said Lager. "Shall we go and collect it then?"

"Let us pass by number three along the way." I proposed. "If there was any reason to have Vicks on hand yesterday, there's even more reason today."

"Oh, yes, quite right, I suppose we ought," stuttered Lager.

"Perhaps peripherally, perhaps not, were you witness to a heartfelt debate between Vicks and Barely Brickstock yesterday?" I asked.

"Why do you ask?"

"Chancy mentioned that he overheard a bit of a bubbly bicker between the scion of the large-scale bond issuing trade and what he describes, with his typically legalistic precision, as 'some woman'."

"Oh, that, yes." Lager glanced to roughly the point in the street that Chancy had identified as the battleground. "I was in the garden, collecting the mail. Why do you ask?"

"Almost entirely speculative. I merely wondered if Vicks had found some source of strength with which to bring a happy end to her fairytale romance."

"I don't think it was Vicks," said Lager. "More likely Miss Belsize and in some fashion related to her sideline in umbrellas."

"I shall doubtless find some inscrutably subtle way to introduce the question into conversation," I said. "Run on ahead, Lager, and warn the tea and biscuits of impending attack. I'll just pop by number three. Vicks won't want to miss the reveal of the Tenpenny Tontine, you know how she admires my acumen."

Miss Belsize was bustling out of number three as I approached, and as our eyes met she levelled on me that wary squint with which I will always associate her — a suspicious sort of grimace that seeks to accuse as defence against accusation. She was less unravelled than when I'd last seen her but, of course, it was early still, and she carried a basket.

"Off to pick posies, Miss Belsize?" I asked. "Should you get lost in the garden — a very real danger — just climb a tree. Assistance will be along presently."

"Got to go to the butchers, don't I?" she answered, with a tone that suggested that going to the butchers was both a tremendous hardship and my doing. "That mongrel's only gone and stolen two pounds of chopped lamb."

"Lucifer has turned to crime?" I said. "I find that difficult to believe. I've observed the character of the animal most carefully, Miss Belsize, and I believe that he would only take that which is explicitly offered, or dropped in the street despite your best efforts."

"Took it right off the counter while my back was turned," insisted the maid.

"I'm heartbroken," I confessed. "I hate to be the one to say it, but you should withdraw his kitchen privileges."

"Who else could have done taken two pounds of raw meat, then?"

"Oh, I don't know," I said, musing. "You didn't notice Mister Brickstock lingering by the service entrance, did you?"

"No," replied Miss Belsize, somewhat vaguely.

"You saw him yesterday, though, didn't you?" I asked. "I understand that you two had words."

"We never did."

"I'm on your side, Miss Belsize," I assured her. "Between you and me, I'm not convinced that Mister Brickstock knows fully how to operate an umbrella."

"I never laid eyes on Mister Brickstock yesterday. Who's saying I did?"

"You've cornered me, Miss Belsize, with your wily *badinage,*" I finally admitted. "Nobody said it. I was guessing. Miss Tenpenny in, by the by?"

Vicks was, indeed, in, and she answered the door on the first bell, as though expecting someone, and her quick countenance of crushing disappointment suggested strongly that it wasn't me. Whoever it was, when he arrived, was in for an eyeful of flapper finery — Vicks was in a pearl-coloured, silky number and her hair was in overlapping curls which formed a dazzling pattern that caused me to briefly lose my balance.

"Mister Boisjoly," she said, as a statement of bald fact. "I had a premonition that it was going to be a bad day."

"How uncanny, so did I, when Vickers — that's my

valet — laid out this very suit. He even got the shoes right. You don't know Vickers, I expect, but if you did you'd know just how ominous that is."

"What can I do for you, Mister Boisjoly?" asked Vicks with just the slightest undertone of unwillingness to actually do anything for me at all.

"I require a chaperone, Miss Tenpenny, for the unveiling of the Tenpenny Tontine. It promises to be the social event of the season and if I make an appearance without a date there'll likely be talk. You know how the society pages are."

Vicks leaned noncommittally against the doorframe. "I thought those two chess masters already established that it was gone for good."

"No, they only determined that it wasn't where they had calculated it to be," I pointed out. "And I think we can agree that this was largely to be expected. The deed to the tontine is still safely at number fifty-seven, and I believe that owing to a natural shyness it won't come out of hiding until a lady is present."

Vicks agreed to accompany me across the square and, in the absence of the Scotts Terrier, I assumed the responsibility of seeing to it that we kept to the sidewalk.

"I apologise, by the way, if I was the cause of any discord between you and Mister Brickstock," I said, striking upon the aforementioned subtle tack.

"And how might you be the cause of any sort of discord between myself and Mister Brickstock?"

"Charm, chiefly," I explained. "I can't seem to turn it off. He gave me to understand that, in his view, I should find a way."

"Are you rich, Mister Boisjoly?"

"Probably. I seem to have rather a lot of things."

"But are you in line to inherit a brokerage house managing millions in City assets?"

"For the sake of the continued good health of City assets," I said, "I sincerely hope not."

"Then you may have no fear in that regard. What made you think that Mister Brickstock and I were not on good terms?"

"I was led to understand that there had been a minor set-to yesterday, here in the square."

"You were misinformed," said Vicks. "Mister Brickstock and I have a most equitable understanding."

"I congratulate you, Miss Tenpenny, and I confess to not a little jealousy," I said. "I hope that I, too, might one day find a soul mate with whom I share the passion of an equitable understanding."

"What I mean to say," Vicks stopped her straight-legged pace to turn and face me outside the door of number fifty-seven, "is that contrary to your information, I have no quarrel with Mister Brickstock. In fact, I have decided to accept his proposal of marriage."


Lager and Chancy were waiting for us in the hall, standing on either side of and looking down at the tile with the crown. Lager was armed once again with his hammer and chisel, and Chancy was nodding sagely.

"All set, Anty," Lager assured me.

"It's under the tile, isn't it?" asked Chancy.

"Amazing we didn't think of it ourselves," answered Lager on my behalf.

"It is, actually, genuinely surprising that you didn't take

up all the tiles and half the garden," I agreed. "But, no, it's not under the tile. It's over it."

"Over it?" Lager and Chancy looked, inexplicably, at each other.

"If I recall correctly, the cryptic clue to the location of the tontine directed us to the crown, indicated by the second archway in the hall, yes?" I asked.

"That's right," said Lager and Chancy together.

"Excellent. And Chancy, I've recently learned that you read architecture at Cambridge."

"And the philosophy thereof, yes," confirmed Lager. "Want to hear me recite *Praktikê?*"

"Keenly," I said. "But at a later date, when I'm at my leisure to give it my fullest attention. In the meantime, I wonder if you might walk us through the constituent parts of an arch, such as that which you see above you?"

Lager and Chancy looked up.

"Oh, let's see, there's your *intrados,* that's the interior radius, corollary to the *extrados,* which is the exterior radius effected by the thickness of the *voussoirs,* which are the wedged blocks forming the arch itself, the centre and typically most prominent of which is the keystone, above which is often, as in this case, the crown..." For a moment Chancy and Lager continued to look up, like baby birds... "Ah. There's a crown."

"There is," I confirmed. "A very handsome and practical example of the genre, too." The crown was formed of progressively extruding layers, like a miniature, reverse staircase, climbing from the top of the archway to the ceiling, but not quite reaching it, leaving a small, almost indiscernible shelf in which one could neatly and permanently store something the rough size and shape of a tontine.

It was judged by all concerned, most encouragingly Vicks, that I was best suited to climb like a circus acrobat onto a delicately balanced construction of two Louis XIV chairs and a piano bench, reach precariously overhead with both hands, and try to wheedle from the crown whatever it was that hid there. In due course and with only a couple of existential moments from which I think I profited spiritually, I withdrew a deep, thin envelope, folded vertically to fit neatly into the crown of an archway.

"Then what was all that business with the tiles and the hidden panel behind the fireplace?" complained Lager as I descended and handed the envelope over to Chancy.

"It was either a clever diversion, planned and implemented over seventy-five years ago," I said, "or it was a coincidence. In light of the fact that the heating at Wedge Hedge Square was, until the turn of the century, coal, followed by gas, followed by electric, it stands to reason that what you interpret as a 'hidden panel' is, in fact, the old coal fireplace, insulated with asbestos when the houses were switched to gas, and the clue of the tiles is merely the legacy of wear and tear over the years repaired with whatever was on hand."

"Oh, yes. Of course," said Lager, in a dazed sort of tone, then composed himself and rubbed his hands together eagerly. "Shall we do this over drinks at number one? Every bag of tea and bottle of tipple seems to have gone missing here. Unless you'd care to host, Vicks?"

"Regrettably, no, I cannot receive you at number three, for the moment," demurred Vicks. "I've run entirely out of tolerance for puerile prattle. I may have more in by the end of the week, but I doubt it."

And so we moved the party to Lager's cosy, two-story Georgian, the interior of which I was seeing for the very first time. It shared a structural aesthetic with number fifty-seven with high ceilings, a long main hall from front-to-back giving onto large, welcoming common areas and punctuated with archways at which we all cast a suspicious eye. It also shared with the larger house a distinctly underfunded aspect — a bit threadbare here, a touch disturbingly mildewed there — and Lager seemed to be hoarding far more than his fair share of dust.

Lager installed us in the salon — very much like the one at number fifty-seven although, obviously, smaller — while he sorted out the tea and biscuits. Chancy sat behind a low parlour table, in the uniform centre of which he lay the envelope, and Vicks and I posed stage-left and stage-right.

Just when there appeared to be some small danger of conversation breaking out, the bells started. First, the Little Ben facsimile on the mantelpiece bonged a single note, to modestly announce that the time now was half-past eleven, in case that was of interest to anyone. Almost simultaneously, Lager wheeled the tea things in on squeaky wheels that tinkled a happy tea-time tune. Then what sounded like a fire alarm went off, creating two distinct camps — Lager and Vicks barely appeared to notice it, and Chancy and I jumped metaphorically out of our skins.

"Must be yours," shouted Lager casually over the din, which was now accompanied by Lucifer who, apparently stimulated by the bells, was yipping a rhythmic accompaniment.

"There's no one at mine. Must be yours," replied Vicks, somehow managing to make a fixture-shuddering roar sound lady-like.

Lager shrugged and set about distributing tea, employing great creativity of mime to communicate 'Sugar? No? Quite sure? Very well, spot of milk, then? Oh, that's right, you take it as it comes. Chancy?'

In time, but nowhere near soon enough, the bells began to subside. Not like the slow, diminishing and distancing church bells of a crisp Sunday morning, but rather like the increasingly infrequent squeals of an infant screaming himself to sleep over some just grievance.

"Ow," said Chancy, massaging each ear with a finger and verbalising what we all felt, I fancy.

"What the devil was that?" I asked.

"Service bell," answered Lager, as though stating an obvious point for the second time. "Very economical and very pointless — you ring a bell in any of the houses, it rings in all the servants' halls. That'll be someone in Vicks' drawing-room, I expect."

"There's nobody at number three," insisted Vicks again. "It's somebody here, in your study."

"There's no one here, either, apart from us."

"Fine." Vicks rose from the divan and put her tea on the tray. "Don't open that till I get back," she said to Chancy, and clipped down the hall and out the front door.

"I'll just make sure it's not Miss Belsize who, having locked herself in the wine cellar again, has resorted to ringing the bell in a blind panic." Lager toodled this as he, too, popped off, leaving Chancy and me to smile vaguely at one another.

"Professionally speaking, Chancy, what do you expect that document to tell you?" I asked, by way of passing the time.

"Not a lot." Chancy looked down at the envelope before him. "It's only the deed — absolutely vital in proving ownership of the original investment, but of course the assets themselves will have mutated and multiplied any number of times and ways since the tontine was first drawn up."

"From whence leads the trail to riches," I ornamented the point, in that charming way I have. "Tell me, Chancy, how do we even know that the Tenpenny Tontine is as wealthy as everyone seems to think it is?"

"It's all a matter of record," said Chancy, shaking his head incongruously. "Any transactions — everything bought and sold and the value thereof — is reported on a quarterly basis to my office."

"So you're still the family solicitor," I surmised.

"Oh, yes, absolutely," said Chancy. "I just have no authority. At all. I'm merely the trustee of record."

"Then who is it who does all the leveraging and diversification and annuity appreciation that I understand is so crucial to the management of a successful portfolio?" I asked.

"Why, any number of City brokerages, I suppose," said Chancy, with child-like wonder in his voice, as though only now was the marvellous enormity of the situation making itself known to him.

"Might this include Brickstock and Son?"

"Seems likely," said Chancy, shaking his head slowly. "They're among the biggest. Rather difficult to avoid, I should think."

This, it soon came to pass, was the length and breadth of Chancy's to-hand knowledge of the financial intricacies of the Tenpenny Tontine, and the next ten minutes or so were consumed with idle speculation about next season's Brooklands, about which Chancy also knew the mathematical equivalent of nothing.

The front door opened and closed and Vicks returned, and footsteps from the service entrance heralded the re-appearance of Lager. Tea was refreshed, biscuits were broken, and the scene was finally set for the opening of the envelope hidden in the crown of the second archway for over seventy-five years.

Chancy repositioned the envelope squarely on the parlour table. He tested the seal, which appeared to have been made of stern stuff. Employing the normally non-combatant end of a teaspoon, Chancy loosened the flap, opened it, and withdrew several thin shafts of paper.

"If anyone's interested," boomed Miss Belsize, who had appeared at the door to the salon quite unexpectedly, "that Brickstock bloke's been murdered."

# CHAPTER TWELVE

# Brickstock's Doom
# in the Same Locked Room

"What do you mean, Brickstock's been murdered?" demanded Lager.

"What do I mean? What do you think I mean?" Miss Belsize struck upon me for support. "Not too many ways to take that, I shouldn't have thought."

"Kimberly's been murdered? He's dead?" said Vicks, stricken in much the same way I've heard first readings of lines like 'Hark, I hear the cannons roar'. "Are you sure?"

"He's in the reading room at number fifty-seven, with a knife in his back." Miss Belsize reported this coolly and without editorial, offering us the bare facts and allowing us to decide for ourselves the gravity of the situation. "And the place looks like a barrel of madeira's been put to waste."

"We must see to him at once," said Lager.

"You'll be lucky." Miss Belsize sighed and trusted the full weight of her shock and fatigue to an underprepared chesterfield fauteuil. "The door's locked."

"You don't meant to say that Brickstock's been

murdered in the reading room, behind a locked door," doubted Lager.

"I do mean to say exactly that," insisted the maid. "The key don't work, neither."

"How could this possibly have happened again?" lamented Lager.

"Well, go to him," exploded Vicks. "There may be something that can be done."

"Ha!" Miss Belsize laughed mirthlessly and poured herself a cup of tea. "Not likely. Going by what I could see through the keyhole, you'd have more luck trying to revive a tinned brisket."

Nevertheless, Lager and I took the initiative, leaving behind the suggestion that someone — ideally Vicks — see about organising some sort of police presence.

≥▲

"A murder," said Ivor, with a withering sort of wonder, "behind locked doors."

"Not to be pedantic, Inspector," I said with that cordial correction that characterises our collaboration, "rather *another* murder, behind the same locked doors."

The inspector and I were outside those very doors, waiting for news from the constable who had been dispatched to the garden-side of the house with a ladder and other tools of the professional break-and-enter artisan.

"They seem to loyally follow you around, locked room murders." Ivor said this with a brave forbearance — the closest he was likely to come to admitting that he probably should have given the suspicious nature of the duel more attention. "You didn't do it, did you?"

"I can see how it would sew things up rather neatly if I had, Inspector, but I regret to say that no, this is unlikely to be settled by a quick confession."

"But you were on hand when it happened."

"So it seems," I said. "The four of us — Lager, Chancy, Vicks Tenpenny, and myself — were here this morning, in the hall."

"Was there anyone in the reading room at the time?" asked Ivor.

"Possibly. The doors were closed," I surveyed the front of the hall from where we stood, "and we were focused on other things. Those other things done, we retired to number one for traditional tea and tontines. Around eleven-thirty somebody, somewhere in Wedge Hedge Square, vigorously and repeatedly yanked the service bell which, incidentally, rings in all three houses."

"I know." Ivor said this with a marvelling sort of tone, as though to acknowledge, 'it is so, and it is odd'. "The maid says that she was in the service hall of number three at the time, and that the bell in question was that of this reading room."

"It stands to reason, then, that this is where and when the murder occurred, although it's hardly conclusive," I said.

Presently, the constable reported in from the other side of the door, in the form of the plinking of breaking glass, an oath of a creative and colourful nature, and the dull thud of man meeting chess-themed floor tile.

"There's quite a bit of blood, Inspector," called a working-class baritone from the other side of the door. "It'll be a bit… messy to get to the door."

"Can't be helped, Constable."

There was much jostling and joggling and jerking open of doors which scraped against the dry, sticky floor, and soon a tall, young, dishevelled constable with no helmet and a dizzy, astonished countenance appeared before us. In his hand was a solid wooden card chair. Behind him was Kimberly Brickstock, not as he'd like to be remembered.

"The door was blocked with this, sir," said the constable referring, without saying so, to the chair. "No way anyone could have gotten in or out."

Though he was clearly a young copper, and green — both in experience and complexion confronting his first death by violence — his analysis of the scene was spot-on — Brickstock was alone in an inaccessible room.

"Clearly he was stabbed in this room and left for dead, but nevertheless managed to barricade the door and ring for help," surmised Ivor, then, "You're fine where you are, Mister Boisjoly," as I endeavoured to follow him into the reading room. "Were you all together when the bell rang?"

"We were," I said. "But Miss Tenpenny and Lager left us briefly to try to determine the source of the commotion."

"Or so they claimed."

"Or so they claimed, indeed, Inspector," I agreed, "but they could hardly have dashed out to put a knife into poor Mister Brickstock if poor Mister Brickstock was already here behind a barricaded door. And prior to that we were none of us out of each other's sight."

"Apart from the maid."

"If Miss Belsize ever turns her hand to serious crime, heaven help the metropolis," I said, "but she doesn't strike me as the murdering kind."

"Who does, among the probable suspects?" Ivor asked, while navigating the wide crimson pool which surrounded the earthly remains of Kimberly Brickstock, like a great tweed island with a knife in its back.

"The dog, I think, given just cause, but he strikes me as the efficient sort of assassin who'd hardly have left his victim in a position to ring for help."

"Any of the human suspects?" clarified Ivor.

"I think that Vicks would probably kill a man for a parking spot," I speculated, "but she was engaged to be married to Mister Brickstock, the poor leaf."

"Not your clubmates, of course."

"You know, Inspector, there's a thin trace of cynicism that comes into your voice when you refer to my place among the vanguard of civilised society," I said coolly. "Club membership is a sacred bond, and core to the very foundations of the nation we both love."

"So, you'll stand by your mates, regardless of their sins."

"Only up to a very specific point," I said. "Sacred bonds are a two-way street and certain codes of behaviour are demanded. This is just an example, you understand, but I was the deciding vote that handed Slippy Bing-ffarrington a six-month suspension from the Juniper for shouting out Prince Henry's punchline at Archbishop Lang's investiture breakfast. Poor chap must have been working on that limerick for months."

"Shall I get the coroner in, Inspector?" asked the constable, who had retreated to the broken window and was affecting to study his handiwork.

"Yes, well done, Constable," said Ivor. "And then get onto Mister Brickstock's last movements." Ivor then turned to me and asked, "Any idea how he got here?"

"I can only say with absolute certainty that he didn't walk," I said. "My guess would be a taxi."

"Off you go then, Constable," said Ivor to the promising young plodder, who made brief, alternating studies of the window and Lake Brickstock before gathering up his helmet, issuing a weak salute, and gingerly exiting by the window.

"Apt chap," I observed. "You neglected to introduce us, incidentally."

"I did, didn't I?" replied Ivor dismissively, less as an answer and more as a sound to make while scrutinising the crime scene. "What's this then?"

Ivor anchored himself on the chair and, from a squatting position, hovered over the last of the Brickstocks. He reached out and plucked from a tweed pocket a crumpled note.

He stood and read it out, "Meet me at once at number fifty-seven. We have much to discuss."

"I don't suppose it's handily signed, is it?"

"It is not, no," said Ivor, turning the note over and examining it from both sides.

"Might I have a look at it?"

Ivor raised his eyebrows indulgently.

"Do you know how you could be most helpful, Mister Boisjoly?" he asked, with the same tone Cook would employ when she put me in charge of the big spoon.

"I do," I said, "but I think we both know it's unlikely I'll be named England Cricket Captain any time soon. I'm probably not even in the running."

"Perhaps you could return to number one and remind

everyone to remain on the premises and not discuss their accounts until they've spoken to me."

I had failed in my mission before it even started. Only Lager and Chancy remained at number one while Vicks, it was reported, had returned home to mourn the loss of her wealthiest suitor and take some sort of inventory of that which remained.

Lager had found in the tragedy cause to break out the Glen Glennegie and, in light of the gravity of the situation, plain water. Chancy was perched with his drink on the divan, cherishing it in that disarming way he has, and Lager was at the mantelpiece, looking at some mail.

"Help yourself, old man," he said. "Do you know a mysterious individual who flies under the curious flag of 'Quiescence Keats'?"

"Let's see." I poured myself a couple of fingers of whisky and a thumbnail of water. "I know so very many people named Quiescence. Would that be the Quiescence Keats who, when not busy harbouring wildly inaccurate prejudices against London, functions as the county clerk of Gutter Folly?"

"The very one. She sent me a letter, and some documents, and mentions you by name." Lager held up the letter for me to view from across the room. "Charmingly misspelt, I might add."

"Quick service," I said. "I only spoke to her the day before yesterday."

"They would have just arrived this morning. They were in the letterbox when we got back. Is this a birth certificate?"

"And a baptismal certificate," I said. "Or at any rate

certified copies thereof, establishing that whatever else he might have been, Ratcliffe Tenpenny was the legally recognised offspring of Terrence Tenpenny."

"I appreciate that, Anty. That'll be a very handy thing to be able to establish in a court of law, should the tontine ever find its way out of probate." Lager knocked the documents into a neat sheaf and laid them on the mantelpiece. "I don't suppose Brickstock's dramatic exit is going to speed up the process any."

From this poor start I did my level best to keep conversation on the path of the mundane — whenever talk veered into speculation about who was where when the bell rang, or whether or not someone could convincingly hide beneath the writing desk in the reading room, I'd give it a good whack in the flanks with idle observations about the weather and the qualities of post-war Glen Glennegie.

So it was both several hours later and not a second too soon that Ivor finally joined us, refused a drink in that officious, abstemious, holier-than-Boisjoly way he has, and said, "One of you is lying."

"Steady on, Inspector," I said. "What makes you say that?"

"You all claim to have not seen Mister Brickstock this morning." Ivor remained by the door and withdrew his pipe from his pocket like a key piece of evidence, followed by his tobacco pouch which he wielded as though it conclusively proved the point made by the pipe. "That seems tremendously unlikely, given that he arrived at the same time you all say you gathered here to search for the tontine."

"Did he?" asked Lager, echoing the room's rising tide

of incredulity. "How could you possibly know that?"

"My constable has identified the cabbie who delivered Mister Brickstock to this address at ten-thirty-five this morning," answered Ivor. "You arrived here after that, I believe you said, Mister Boisjoly?"

"Eleven-ish, I'd say."

"And Mister Proctor?" Ivor asked of Chancy, who appeared unprepared for the question.

"Oh, about then, I suppose."

"And Mister Tenpenny?"

"I live here, Inspector," said Lager with deliberate indifference, as one deigning to point out the obvious.

"Doubtless we just missed him," I said. "Might have been hiding in the garden. You didn't know the man the way we did, Inspector — timid as a spring fawn — or... did you?"

"Did I what?" Ivor lit his pipe with a cold deliberation, like a surgeon with a scalpel, or a seasoned barman with a quarter ounce of vermouth.

"Did you know Mister Brickstock?" I clarified. "He said that he planned to confer with you on a matter of some importance regarding the murder in the reading room of number fifty-seven... the previous murder in the reading room of number fifty-seven, of course I mean."

"What matter?"

"That I could not say, Inspector," I despaired. "He alluded to subjects beyond my ken, which, candidly, is a rather broad field."

"Any idea what he meant?" Ivor asked of Chancy and Lager, who shared a glance and then replied with synchronised head shaking.

"You might ask Victoria Tenpenny, or Miss Belsize," I suggested. "Brickstock was overheard in spirited dialogue with one or the other."

"I say, Inspector, you don't suppose..." Lager introduced this dramatic prompt like he expected it to be accompanied by something by Prokofiev.

"...that Miss Tenpenny or Miss Belsize murdered Mister Brickstock?" completed Ivor. "I think not. The coroner has just examined the body, and has determined that the attack was, in his words, 'comprehensive'. Mister Brickstock was stabbed in the abdomen prior to receiving what turns out to have been a superfluous blow to the back."

"That would explain the uncanny resemblance the reading room of number fifty-seven bears to a Victorian abattoir."

"Just so." Ivor drew on his pipe meditatively before elaborating. "Babbage says that the amount of blood lost was such that, by the time the knife was driven home the for final time, Brickstock would have had seconds to live."

"How... vivid." I topped up my whisky from the bottle and, in view of the solemnity of the occasion, added no water. "Returning to this fascinating cabbie, Inspector, was he able to provide an exact address?"

"He just said that he dropped off Mister Brickstock at the gate to Wedge Hedge Square."

"Indeed, this is what I assumed," I said, "but I wasn't referring to the destination, Inspector. I was asking about the departure point, which we can assume was not Mister Brickstock's home."

"And how can we assume that?" The Inspector is a consummate professional and hence didn't actually precede the question with 'Oh, yeah?' but it was clearly implied.

"The note, Inspector," I explained. "It's hand-written, and unsigned. Brickstock's butler is hardly going to accept never mind deliver an anonymous missive. It wasn't his club, either, I'll wager, for the same reason. No, the note which lured Brickstock here was dictated by telephone to the *maitre d'* of a restaurant which, given the hour and consequent fact that they do breakfast, is that of an hotel. The Savoy?"

"Claridge's," said Ivor, as one folding his hand.

"Claridge's. Of course. Their pastry chef has a *Legion d'Honneur.*"

"Very well, Mister Boisjoly. I appreciate the insight. I'll visit Claridge's when I'm done here."

"I think that it should be as soon as possible, Inspector," I said. "Staff turnover in these places is of a frequency rivalling the third act of *A Midsummer Night's Dream.* I've personally seen three sommeliers and two captains rotated out at the Ritz, and that was just one Sunday brunch."

"Noted."

"And, of course, I should go with you."

"That won't be necessary, thank you, Mister Boisjoly." Ivor waggled his pipe stem in a simple semaphore.

"Not strictly necessary, no," I conceded. "But delightfully chummy. And Claridge's is my indigenous land. My people. My caste and cadence. You'll need an interpreter, at the very least, and I may notice something that you miss, such as the significance of the note, or the footprints."

"Footprints?" Ivor looked up, now, for he had been carefully studying his pipe as I spoke. "What footprints?"

"Precisely my point, Inspector. Earlier you contended

that the murder of Kimberly Brickstock was no locked room mystery, and that he'd merely locked himself into the reading room after being stabbed, but now we know that the pool of blood between the body and the door preceded the knife in the back. That being the case, how did the killer leave the room without leaving bloody footprints?"

# CHAPTER THIRTEEN

# The Meagre Wage
# of the Pithy Page

Claridge's, in the gilded heart of Mayfair, is the king of hotels and the hotel of kings. It's the bright-bricked, baroque, bay of solace to which one retreats when the common proletariat of the smoking rooms of the Ritz and tea parlours of Rubens come over all the huddled mass, and the only possible tonic is a Mcallan 1860 and naturally effervescent Galvanini spring water from the very peak of San Lorenzo Mountain served in a hand-blown lead crystal highball by a man who's been training to do so all his life.

I'd deny it under oath, but to me Claridge's has always been a bit dreary. I understand that plans are afoot to change all that and that's a very fine thing because as it is the hotel looks more like a dusty museum of the Belle Epoque than it does London's premier doss-bin for European royalty. It is what it is, though, and it's conservatively estimated that were the place ever hit by a bomb or a raging case of ptomaine poisoning half the nations of the world would have to change their postage stamps.

Of course I shared all this with Ivor before we arrived, so he was a bouncy balance of nervous quivering and resolute egalitarianism by the time the doorman, to whom Ivor tipped his hat, bowed us through.

"You really think the king will be here?" asked Ivor discreetly out the side of his mouth.

"Certainly *a* king will be here," I assured him. "They stock them by the half-dozen here at Claridge's. It's said that during the war they were stacking them in bunk-beds and referring anything less than prince consort to the Ritz."

There's always something of an air of a refugee crossroads about the lobby of Claridge's. It's a frenzy, like Waterloo Station on Christmas eve, but with fewer carollers and more chaps dressed like Saint Nick. Today was a particularly chaotic zigging of pages and zagging of porters through a zoo of nobility. Ivor took in the blur of uniforms and tuxedos and gowns and robes of religious and regional and regimental relevance with a dazzled countenance that put me in mind of my first time seeing the foyer of the famous hotel, when I hid behind my father's greatcoat until Lord Landsdowne offered me a puff of his cigar.

Claridge's restaurant was a relative sanctuary of calm, still anticipation of the gathering storm of teatime. Commis staff in black waistcoats and terrified expressions were polishing silver and folding napkins and laying out tables in the complex code of single-purpose cutlery, invented by the French as a sort of culinary shibboleth to identify and mock those who have better things to do with their time. Tall windows gleamed, chandeliers glittered from high overhead, the copper-threaded wallpaper twinkled, silverware shone, crisp, white tablecloths glowed and floor-to-ceiling mirrors glimmered it all back on itself, multiplying the effect and making the hall appear even bigger and brighter and grander than it was.

At the entrance, manning a podium like it was the bridge of a ship of state, was a statuesque mortician who appeared to have been carved in place, like the cherubs at the tops of the mirror frames.

"Good afternoon," said Ivor to the maitre d'. "I'm Inspector Wittersham of Scotland Yard. This is Mister Boisjoly. In pursuant of a serious police enquiry I require some information about one of your guests who was here this morning."

The mortician, who had managed to make even his bowtie look dour, slowly raised an eyebrow. It was an impressively lengthy ordeal. I'm not certain, if called upon to do so, I could have held my breath that long.

"Indeed, sir?" he said, less as a question and more as a variation of 'Think so, do you?' expressed in fluent, accentless Claridge's.

"Kimberly Brickstock," continued Ivor, unaware that he was already being stone-walled and no mistake about it. "He would have received a message at his table."

"I was not on duty this morning, sir," replied the maitre d', and then turned his attention to sorting his identical black pens by colour.

"Tell you what, Inspector," I said. "How about I stand you a high tea at Claridge's? I feel I still owe you from that time you didn't arrest me."

"Have you a reservation, sir?" asked the maitre d' with that flat, rhetorical certainty that I did not.

"I never make reservations," I said. "It only ever leads to disappointment and heartbreak. Is anyone occupying Viscount Broadgate's table?"

"And you are?"

"Anthony Boisjoly. Son of Edmond. Direct descendant of Eadbert the Tardy."

The mortician's eyes fluttered down to the reservation book, like the wings of one of the more patronising species of butterfly. When they fluttered back to the surface they were agleam with respectful recognition.

"For two, Mister Boisjoly?"

"Unless you'd care to join us."

"If you'll follow me, gentlemen."

"Take my friend to the table," I said to our guide, "and beguile him with tales of salmon smoked in the fumes of rare woods and the coddled eggs of coddled hens stuffed with the caviar of hand-raised sturgeon. I have to make quick use of the telephone."

By the time I returned, only minutes later, Ivor was in a state of stunned immobility brought on, by all appearances, by the existence of a tall champagne flute brimming with effervescence and ornamented with an orchid.

"How did that come into being?" I asked, taking my seat next to Ivor, so that we were both surveying the restaurant.

"I don't know," he said, still studying the monstrosity. "A man in a tuxedo spoke to me in, I think, French, and somehow we negotiated this. I don't even know what it is."

"Elderflower champagne cordial," I explained. "You're starting strong out of the gate, Inspector. Most of us don't order champagne for tea at Claridge's until we've rehearsed a few breakfast cocktails at the club."

The captain returned and gave us menus and took my order for lashings of Darjeeling.

"What are 'wheaters'?" asked Ivor.

"It's pronounced *'huitres'*," I said. "Oysters. A fixture of high tea at Claridge's. It's often said that what cheese straws are to Pinoli's, oysters are to Claridge's. For professionals only — they're alive when you eat them, you understand, and probably for some unknowable time afterward, too."

"How many do you get for six shillings?"

"That's per oyster."

"Blimey."

The mortician was ferrying parties to surrounding tables and a proper tea-time din began to raise the tone of the place. At the door, several potentates waited bovinely, and between them materialised a pageboy in red jacket and pillbox hat over a straw-blond mop and a freckled dial. He conferred with the maitre d', briefly, cast an eager eye in our direction, and then sped over.

"Inspector Wittersham?" said the lad, who would have been about fourteen years old but with the cynical, jaded bearing of one who's made his own way in life.

"Yes?" answered Ivor guardedly.

The boy raised a silver salver, on which rested a folded note.

"Message for you, sir."

Ivor took the paper tentatively, unfolded it, and read it out.

"It says, 'Don't order the oysters'."

"I know," I said. "I sent it. I wanted to spare you the embarrassment of asking what they were. It came too late."

"Begging your pardon, sir, I come as soon as the message was given me," said the page in quick defence of his reputation — the stock and trade of the Mayfair page.

"Stout lad," I said. "I assumed as much. That is, in fact, the real reason I sent the message and, between you and me, I very much hope that the inspector here *does* order the oysters — they pair so well with champagne cordials. We wished only to make your acquaintance. I'm Mister Boisjoly, and you are?"

"Busy, sir, delivering real messages."

"Besides that, I mean."

"Richard Purdy. Friends call me Chard."

"I hope to be counted among your closest, Chard," I said. "Tell me something, were you working here this morning?"

"Yes, sir."

"Excellent. And did you deliver a message to a Mister Brickstock?"

"I did, sir, yes sir."

"And what do you recall of it?" asked Ivor.

"I recall that the gentleman neglected to give me a tip, sir."

"Ah, yes, of course," said Ivor. He glanced nervously at me and then produced a mediaeval change purse, with a draw-string. From it, he withdrew a penny, and placed it on the boy's tray.

"Oh, bless you, sir," said Chard, smiling down on the penny. "You couldn't see your way clear to making it two pennies, could you sir? Then I could buy back the family estate in Harrow."

"Now listen here, young man, this is a police matter," said Ivor with firm authority.

"Good living, is it, this policing lark?" asked Chard, leaning on a chair. "'Cause I can tell you sir, I make a solid packet delivering messages and collecting penny tips."

"I'll see you don't lose out by it, Chard," I assured him. "From whom did the message come?"

"Desk clerk, I think." Chard looked back toward the door and beyond to the foyer. "I never seen her before. She just handed me a message and told me to give it to Mister Brickstock, who was over there, at that table." Chard nodded toward a corner table which in that moment was occupied by the Lord Privy Seal and, let us say, his daughter.

"How did they know that Mister Brickstock was dining here?" asked Ivor.

"You'll hardly credit it, sir," said Chard with wonder in his voice. "but I neglected to ask the lady how it was the person what left the message for Mister Brickstock knew that he was here. I'm still kicking myself for it, sir. Amateur oversight, really."

"Could you point out the woman who gave you the note?" asked Ivor with the studied patience of the professional interrogator.

"I could," said Chard, "if she were here, which she ain't. I never seen her before nor since."

"When Mister Brickstock read the message, then," exasperated Ivor, "did he give any indication that he knew who it was from?"

"He didn't read it, sir."

"That's curious," I opined. "I wonder why not?"

"Because he was otherwise occupied," explained Chard, "with a plate of scones as big as his head, a half-pound of creamery butter, a stack of crêpes and strawberries, and a basket of sticky buns. He had me read it to him."

"I expect that we know already, but do you recall what the note said?" I asked.

"Of course I do, sir," said Chard earnestly. "I scrupulously record all the messages that I deliver. My fondest pastime of an evening, when I'm not at my club, is to carefully catalogue my collection of correspondence in the hope of one day making a significant contribution to the Oxford Department of English Letters."

I put ten shillings on his tray and Chard poured the coins into a front pocket of his waistcoat. He put his hands behind his back and looked to the sky, on which we write memories.

"It said, 'Meet me at once at number fifty-seven. We have much to discuss.'"

"Then what did Mister Brickstock do?" asked Ivor.

"Put the note in his pocket. Told me to get him a taxi straight away." Chard reproduced and gazed nostalgically at his silver salver. "And I'm not sure if I mentioned it, sir, but the gentleman neglected to tip."


I'd like to report that tea with Ivor at Claridge's was a slap-up binge for the history books, buoyed on booze and boisterous bonhomie, but that would be something of a departure from the truth. As the afternoon unfolded, Ivor's frenetic fluster in the face of such overwhelming numbers of nibs and nobility became very much the theme of the occasion. He ordered parsimoniously, he ate sparingly, and he endeavoured to take the edge off with dangerous gulps of elderflower champagne cordial. The high point, or at any rate the moment that will most vividly remain in our memories, was when the Duke of Kent came in wearing full dress uniform and Ivor leapt to his feet with such alacrity that he upset a dessert trolly and the delicate feelings of a *maitre fromager*. Afterwards, I had to take him to the Navvy and Spade where he required two pints of honest bitter to remember he was an Englishman.

We parted company at Hyde Park, through which I walked and brooded on that which we'd learned. I brooded all the way to Kensington and I brooded over an excellent pink lamb chop and purée of potato and chives with a Château de Meursault '18, the brooding man's burgundy, and then I brooded off to bed.

I awake heavily, as a rule. Dreamily and just beneath the waves, like a jellyfish — sometimes rising near the surface of lucidity only to slip away again into the deeps. With each ebb and flow, reality makes itself known to me in small, genial gestures. Here's a little sunlight diffused by the curtains, followed by a return to that dream in which I'm sleeping in a meadow surrounded by rabbits, then a church bell rings, back to the rabbits, and by and by Vickers is there, with a breakfast tray.

These are just examples, of course. Often there are lambs instead of or in addition to rabbits, and rarely does Vickers manage to correspond breakfast to morning. Likely as not, he'll lay out my swallowtails and wheel in the drinks tray, but this morning his *mise-en-place* were *mises* in almost all the right *places*.

"I say, Vickers," I said, as colour commentary to the spectacle of a trained professional peeling a hard-boiled egg. "Have you forgotten your trousers?"

"No, sir," replied Vickers, without skipping a beat of the teaspoon against the shell, "I have mislaid them."

"Right-ho. Doubtless it'll be all the rage among gentlemen's personal gentlemen, just as soon as you're spotted about town in your fetching striped *culottes* and suspenders. Is that a telegram?" I referred to the fold of paper occupying the fourth and remaining slot of the toast rack.

"It arrived this morning, sir, from a Mister Chauncy Proctor." Vickers handed over a steaming cup of empire, just as it comes from the pot.

"Recite it to me, will you Vickers. I still have rabbit meadow eyes."

Vickers carried the telegram to the light of the window and read out loud in a toneless, telegram voice, "Rummiest thing in amongst tontine papers… Also rummier thing still in post this morning… Could stand a bit of the Boisjoly bean for either… Both really… I say... never mind all that... could you just pop by the office at your earliest re rummy thing... Best... Chancy."

"Rummy," I observed.

"Indeed, sir. Would you care to send a reply?"

"No, I think not. Chancy is best appreciated in person, like Punch and Judy, he loses most — though evidently not all — of the charm on paper." I held my cup aloft as Vickers positioned the breakfast tray. "Lay out my Deerstalker and Meerschaum, Vickers and, if you have any on hand, slap on a wizened Bloodhound or two. I feel that today the trail is sizzling hot. By the way, Kimberly Brickstock was murdered yesterday."

"This is most disturbing to hear."

"Somebody had to tell you."

"In fact, I believe that someone already made me aware of the regrettable development." Vickers looked inquisitively skyward. "He died in a duel, if memory serves."

"It very nearly does, Vickers old birthright," I said. "But you're thinking of the previous murder, and it was I who broke the story of the demise of the last of what the smart set are calling the Tontine Generation."

Vickers focused hard on a spot somewhere in the middlefield.

"Don't let it torment you," I reassured him. "The details don't make it any less confounding. Mister Brickstock died in similar circumstances — he was stabbed in a locked room. It was, probably not coincidentally, the very same room; the reading room at number fifty-seven Wedge Hedge Square, otherwise known as the most dangerous room in London, after the fragrance counter at Selfridges."

"And he was entirely alone?"

"Manifestly not," I said, bookmarking a wobbly bit of yolk with a toasty soldier. "But whoever provided the stabbing service somehow escaped the room over a six-foot pool of blood, without so much as dipping a toe in. There were no footprints in the hall."

"Presumably the killer removed his shoes after walking through the blood."

This observation froze a dripping bit of toast on its way to fulfilling its calling.

"Well, I'll be dangled," I declared. "I hadn't thought of that."

"Doubtless owing to a quality upbringing," said Vickers, munificently. "A gentleman doesn't go about the common areas of the home in stockinged feet."

"Yes, that must be it. In any case, it still would've required extraordinary dexterity on the part of the killer — assuming all is as it appears, Mister Brickstock managed to bar the door, ring for assistance, and expire, all in a matter of seconds, while his assailant danced to safety. They'd almost have had to rehearse it. And, as has become tradition at number fifty-seven, Wedge Hedge Square, all the viable suspects, with the exception of the redoubtable-but-not-quite-that-redoubtable Miss Belsize, were together when the curtain fell on Mister Brickstock."

"And there were no witnesses?"

"There were not," I said, and then mused momentarily, aided in the act with a bit of sausage. "Actually, in a manner of speaking, there may have been. I've just now recalled that seconds after the service bell started ringing I heard the unmistakable song of the city-born terrier — Lucifer the Scottish Cerberus was expressing a dissenting opinion in his characteristically candid manner."

"It seems unlikely that no one even saw Mister Brickstock arrive."

"A taxi delivered him to the front gate of Wedge Hedge Square, to which he was summoned by anonymous note, delivered by sarcastic page, rendered by mysterious woman at Claridge's."

"Claridge's?" Vickers is always impressed by any mention of Claridge's, the Carlton Club, or the Hogarth, which closed in 1861.

"Yes, Claridge's," I confided, "but if you see Viscount Broadgate in the near term, deny everything. Now, to the bath, Vickers, and let us discover this new twist in the tale of the Tenpenny Tontine."

ॐ

The City of London, by which I mean that which is referred to as the Square Mile enclave of capital and commerce in the centre of the centre of the world, always makes me feel under-rehearsed. It's the stark staginess of the place, I think — it's what London would look like if it had been built specifically as scenery. There are loads of lovely lines and complex compositions and Wrens and Sloanes and who-have-yous, but it's all so clean and quiet and devoid of people, particularly during the hours when I find myself there, that it puts me in mind of Eton and my catastrophic turn as Falstaff in *Henry V,* when I'd understudied Falstaff in *The Merry Wives of Windsor.*

The office of the Proctor family firm of solicitors is and always has been on Lombard Street, a narrow, ancient, delightful mish-mash of stone buildings that survived the Great Fire, elaborate churches rebuilt since, columned banks and brokerages, archways, porte-cocheres, and, possibly best of all, all manner of eccentric signage, depicting everything from brass crickets to musical cats and whatever could reasonably be described as 'in-between' those extremes.

I had never been to Chancy's office prior to that day but I'd been led to understand that they had once been magnificent, occupying two floors above a famed tea shop, denoted by a real porcelain cup the size of a bathtub suspended above the entrance. Now, Proctor and Proctor, as it was still called, had been reduced to a two-room office with a high arched window overlooking the teacup.

"Hullo Anty." Chancy hailed me cheerfully from behind a desk no smaller than a grand piano at the far end of a room no larger than a concert hall. It was an unnervingly symmetrical sort of room, neatly divided by high panels, like the columns of an accountancy book, and each column was headed with a portrait of a Proctor predecessor above a filing cabinet. As the columns approached the desk the portraits grew more modern in execution and more like Chancy in distance between the eyes, and the cabinets became newer and neater and, I expect, emptier.

"Hallo!" I called back, waving from the distant door. "I'm over here."

"I hope you don't want tea or anything, Anty," said Chancy as I made the journey toward his end of the room. "We don't really have water or any manner of heating it up. Or tea, really."

"Think nothing of it Chancy old trout, my man saw me off fully irrigated," I said and, breathless, took one of two leather armchairs on the mug's side of the vast, acutely organised desk. "He also read me your telegram which, I'd like to say, went from strength to strength."

"Rummiest thing, Anty." Chancy placed a hand on a brown paper parcel which I took to be, from the size and shape, a hatbox. "It arrived this morning, care of this office, attention Kimberly Brickstock."

"Who is it from?"

"No idea." Chancy turned the top of the box toward me so that I could read the address: 'In care of Proctor and Proctor, to be held unsealed on behalf and at the direction of Mister Kimberly Brickstock.'

"What should I do with it?" asked Chancy. "I mean, what with Brickstock being dead and what not."

"Sounds a slippery legal point," I said. "Were it me, Chancy, I'd ask a solicitor."

"Yes, I take your point, Anty, but it's not just property, is it? Might be evidence, too. What do you think I should do?"

"After considering the matter carefully, Chancy, I think you should open it."

"I can't do that." Chancy withdrew his hand from the package as though it had suddenly burst into flames.

"Doesn't look very complicated," I said. "Just some paper and a bit of string. That knot looks a bit tricky, but if you have a knife, or sturdy letter-opener..." I took up the box and gave it a little Christmas eve shake. "Bet you it's not books."

"You really think we should open it?"

"Not much choice, now, is there Chancy — we have a bet to settle."

"I really don't think the inspector would approve."

"That's because you don't know him the way I do, Chancy old man," I said. "I know for a fact he won't approve. But I'll bring the box to the inspector, once we've satisfied your adamantine curiosity."

I put the box on the desk and untied the twine and peeled off the paper. It was indeed something very like a hat box but when I removed the lid I found quite the opposite.

"Are those ladies' shoes?" asked Chancy, presumably rhetorically, because there was nothing else they could have been — a pair of Cuban-heeled strap pumps in two-toned brown leather.

I withdrew them from the box and, pursuing the instinct that comes to all men when judging shoes, I turned them over.

"Is that..." began Chancy.

"Yes, there's no mistaking," I said, "there's blood on the sole of this shoe."

In that same moment, a pleasingly familiar voice sang

166

from the door, "Mister Proctor? Mister Chauncy Proctor?"

And there stood Quiescence 'Quip' Keats.

# CHAPTER FOURTEEN

# The Mainly Moderate Metals Market

I dropped the shoes into the box and put the lid back on.

"Anty?" Quip squinted at me across the vast frontier. "Is that you?"

"I was about to ask you something uncannily similar."

Quip had dressed for London with a keen eye on the possibility that the coronation of Edward VII might have to be restaged. Turn-of-the-century inflatable shoulders and immersive decolletage hadn't looked so fetching in thirty years, and her hair was mangled into a playful parody of a Parisian plait. She was, in short, a divine maximum of what a woman can be when she doesn't give a ham sandwich what London fashion thinks of her.

"This is the other rummy thing I was going to mention, Anty," said Chancy, who had stood now as a lady approached. "There were some bequests in the envelope with the tontine."

"Bequests? From whom? *For* whom?"

"Ratcliffe and Hadley Tenpenny, and a woman called Willow Willoughby."

"Miss Keats' grandmother," I added. "And the bequest is from Terrence Tenpenny, I take it, in recognition of her care for his illegitimate son."

"Ratcliffe Tenpenny," guessed Chancy.

"Correct," I confirmed. "Miss Keats' grandmother was his nanny."

"Well, that explains that," said Chancy. "I sent a telegram to the address in the bequest; Drab House, Drab-on-Drabble."

"And I answered," completed Quip, with a giddy sort of undertone, as though bursting with a positively mortal punchline.

"Please, Miss Keats, take a seat," swooned Chancy. "May I offer you tea?"

"No, thanks very much," said Quip. Subconsciously determined to continue winning my heart, she added, "I never take tea while the pubs are open."

"Quite sure? I haven't actually got any, as it goes, but I expect I could pop downstairs and purchase the necessaries."

"Very kind, but no."

"When I got Miss Keats' reply," explained Chancy, suddenly remembering to sit down, "I recalled that you had mentioned her name to Lager."

"This Lager," said Quip to me, "is he an actual chap, or were you discussing me with your pint?"

"Actual chap," I replied. "One of the candidates for the generous inheritance that I mentioned."

"More than happy to share, especially with anyone named Lager." Quip clutched her oversized handbag and leaned enthusiastically toward Chancy. "I can't tell you how much this means to us, Mister Proctor. Drab House is in a dreadful state — effectively uninhabitable. This bequest will mean comfortable, dignified retirement for countless deserving smugglers and con artists." Quip smiled benevolently at me. "We'll sort out a good home for the bats, too."

I basked in Quip's happiness for her grandmother and the smugglers with whom she shared 1867 until I looked back at Chancy, whose gape-mouthed stupor foretold of sad tidings. Quip saw it, too, but opted for the more agreeable interpretation that Chancy was having some sort of fit.

"Is he okay?" she asked me out of the side of her mouth.

"I… there may have been some misunderstanding, Miss Keats," said Chancy, finally. "The bequest is not a share of the Tenpenny Tontine. It's a separate legacy established by Terrence Tenpenny himself, in 1885."

"I see," said Quip guardedly. "And what is the nature of this legacy?"

Chancy contrived to form a smile, of sorts, that instead gave him the countenance of one pretending to not be drunk before a magistrate. He pulled open a drawer of his desk and withdrew the envelope that we'd found in the crown of the second archway in the hall of number fifty-seven. From this, he produced several sheets of thick certificate paper.

"These are instructions to my grandfather." Chancy held up one of the papers to illustrate the point. "Mister Tenpenny wanted to discourage rivalry between the generation that would dissolve the tontine — possibly he anticipated just such an eventuality as has come to pass." Chancy turned his twisted smile briefly on me, as a silent plea for support. "He set aside one hundred pounds each — a very substantial sum in 1885, you understand — to be invested in some safe financial instrument, the interest of which was to compound annually."

"Oh, I see." Quip put both hands on the side of the desk as though to stabilise herself after this near-miss. "Well, that's all right then. I don't need a fortune, Mister Proctor, just enough to fix up the roof, maybe lay on some heat. The bats can stick on a bit longer, if they like."

"This safe, interest-bearing financial instrument of which you speak, Chancy," I began warily, as one deliberately setting foot on a frozen river at the crack of spring thaw. "What did your grandfather choose?"

"Gold."

"Gold?" The word appeared to cheer and confuse Quip in equal measure. "That's good, isn't it? Everyone needs gold for whatever it is people need gold for. Teeth or something, isn't it?"

Of course, Quip didn't know the Proctor family reputation for constantly and quickly taking hold of the sticky end, so it was left to me to dread the next few moments on her behalf.

"Yes," continued Chancy tentatively. "My grandfather bought a hundred pounds' of gold on your grandmother's behalf."

"A hundred pounds!"

"A hundred pounds' worth, I should say," clarified Chancy, as he often finds himself doing. "About twenty-three and a half ounces, at the time."

"I see." Quip's smile tried gamely to keep up appearances, but one could see it was struggling. "And how much is that worth now?"

"Ah, uhm…" Chancy withdrew a pencil from his jacket

pocket and scratched a simple formula on the envelope. "About... oh, let's see... ninety-nine pounds fifteen and thruppence."

"Ninety-nine pounds..." Quip repeated this flatly.

"...fifteen and thruppence," continued Chancy. "It's really held its value, gold. Stability, I expect, was the key feature of the instruction, in my grandfather's view."

Quip's Parisian plait depleted. Her shoulders deflated. Only her slim, steely smile held the course, unaware that a shimmering great tear streamed toward it at the speed of sorrow. She held her chin up, though, and stared ahead, past Chancy and the giant teacup and Lombard Street and the City of London and all the way to the crumbling, hopeless sanctuary in Gutter Folly.

Chancy and I shared a helpless glance.

"The good news, Quip, is that you're sat next to one of the great roof-building fortunes of England," I blurted. "I've probably contributed to more lids of country churches than there are country churches, I can certainly manage an economy-sized retirement shelter."

Quip squeezed her eyes closed, briefly, and touched away the overflow with a gloved hand, but continued to focus on Drab House.

"That's very kind, Mister Boisjoly," she said, employing the formal address as, I expect, a point of pride. "There are bats living in the dining room, you know. One of them flew into a mirror on the second-floor landing only this week, and was knocked to the floor. It fell through." She wiped her cheeks again, this time bringing much-needed reinforcements in the form of a lace handkerchief. "The entire northeast tower is at the bottom of a swamp. A new sinkhole has opened up in the apple orchard, swallowing a Ribston Pippin and a potting shed." Finally she turned to face me. "I have no intention of wasting a pound of a good man's fortune on a lost cause." Quip dabbed her eyes once more, and somehow willed the tears to cease. She smiled a sardonic, laughing-at-my-own-misfortune smile. "Tell me, gentlemen, why is it that men are so very good at wasting money?"

Chancy and I shared another meaningful glance. In my case, I was telegraphing the obvious; 'Jolly good question, that — why *are* we so good at wasting money?' I mean to say, I'd never given it much consideration until then, but in my experience it's an area in which women as a class tend to fail spectacularly. Chancy's mind, it turns out, was on more spiritual matters. He rose — quietly and discreetly, as though sneaking out of church during the homily — and slipped to a nearby filing cabinet. He opened the second drawer — one of those ingenious folding-out numbers that doubles as a little writing desk — and withdrew three snifters and a bottle of brandy.

"Thank you, Mister Proctor," said Quip, taking the offered glass.

"Please, call me Chauncy."

"Why are men such squanderers, Chauncy?" Quip drank deeply of her brandy and handed the empty back for a refill. "Smuggling's a good business, you know, done right. Thank you." She received the refreshed snifter. "Gutter Folly was actually thriving, for a goodish bit of time, my nan tells me. They just needed to put a bit away, for the future, for the unforeseen — roof repairs, to seize upon an obvious example — instead of drinking it or buying boats that get impounded by the French authorities who chuck you in prison for a month." Quip raised her glass in a toast. "To my dear father!"

Dashed difficult thing it is, responding to a sarcastic toast. Like one of those, loaded, 'do you still cheat at Backgammon?' sort of arrangements. Chancy and I, naturally, settled on the worst possible combination of the choices to hand — we raised our glasses but didn't drink. Quip drained her glass.

"If your father's encountered difficulties with the armagnac shipment, there's no hurry," I assured her. "I have plenty to see me through."

"I'm sure he has." Quip regarded her snifter like a crystal ball which revealed a thousand stories, none of which held any interest for her at all. "Likely he's scuttled his boat with the entire stock on board. Or drunk it all and run aground at Southend-on-Sea, having missed the mouth of the river Drabble by two hundred miles. Again." Quip laughed that mirthless, fatalistic snort that I hear so often at the casino when the dealer draws twenty-one for the twelfth time running. "It's the only lasting tradition we have in Gutter Folly, really. There are a couple of codgers at Drab House still, to this day, trying to recover the investment they made in hand-rolled cigarettes right about the time the process became fully automated. Stow, the butler, trifled away a fortune backing musical theatre. And when my own father came into his little all the first thing he did was buy a boat and sail it to Calais where he mistook two French customs officials for wine merchants."

"Easy mistake to make," I said, "the uniform is virtually identical."

"He was twenty-one," mused Quip. "Since then he's donated some four steam tugs and an ocean-going trawler to the French authorities. Can I have my ninety-nine pounds fifteen and thruppence now, please, Chauncy? I'll need to get it into the bank before my father is able to use it to purchase a hot-air balloon."

"In point of fact, Miss Keats, I didn't realise that your father and grandmother were still, ehm, pertinent," said Chancy, with all the diplomatic syrup he could produce on short notice. "I'm afraid that I'll need instructions from Miss Willoughby."

"I have power of attorney," said Quip. "My father is never in one place long enough to manage his mother's affairs, or his own, if it comes to that, and she's incapable of advising a solicitor."

"I can attest to that, Chancy," I added. "I've met Miss Willoughby — delightful old bird but she's definitely viewing reality through several jars of marmalade."

"Are you remaining in London, Miss Keats?" asked Chancy, smiling perhaps more naturally, now — less like a drunk trying to appear sober and more like a drunk trying to appear suave.

"Call me Quip."

"Quip…" Chancy repeated this the way one pronounces 'chocolate mousse' the first time one learns of its existence.

"I must get back to Gutter Folly," said Quip, rising and gathering herself. "After dark many of the residents of Drab House need to be watched, or they'll stumble into the swamp or try to walk to France."

"I'll need until tomorrow to liquidate your assets, Quip," Chancy stopped here to giggle briefly but hysterically, "I'd be very happy to deliver you a cheque personally."

"I suppose I could stay at the hotel by the station."

"Allow me to accompany you…" This was said in a lovely a capella, Chancy providing the tenor and I, naturally, the baritone. We looked at each other with forced cordiality.

"You have office hours to keep, Chancy old man," I said. "I'll take Quip to the station."

"I have no other appointments today, Anty old chap," replied Chancy, his hands up in a 'oh, don't trifle yourself gesture'. "And Quip and I may have other business to discuss."

"Do you even know how to get to Liverpool Street, Chancy?" I asked, hands on hips, now, and kid gloves off.

"Doubtless the cabbie will require little guidance," said Chancy with measured hauteur. "And in any case…" He glanced down at the hatbox. "…I believe you have an important engagement with Inspector Wittersham."

❧

Chance is a funny sort of thing. I don't mean so much the odds of any horse I put my last collar stud on retiring to private life before the first hurdle — that's broadly accepted as a universal constant of exactly nineteen to two — but rather that unknowable rippling of circumstance, so often characterised by your boffins as one grain of sand quite innocently shifting and causing all manner of bother for another grain of sand the next beach over, even if the two had never met socially. Take what came to be a very telling lunch at the Juniper, which wouldn't have happened had I not been outmanoeuvred by Chauncy the Chancy Lawyer, of all people, and hence not felt just that persecuted that I merited a measure of cold roast beef and claret before facing Inspector Wittersham. As it happens the Juniper is, give or take a wrong turn, right on the way to Scotland Yard.

And so I found myself tripping down a Mayfair boulevard to my club, distracted by trying or not trying to step on every crack in the sidewalk (I can't recall which and it's actually not that relevant to what happened next) when I looked up and who should I see coming down the steps of the Juniper but Dial Crocker, of the Swashbucklers Society membership committee. He had a pinched, distracted sort of air about him — or at any rate that which I could see of his face behind his hibiscus moustache and boot-brush eyebrows looked pinched and distracted — as though he was meant to do something important but forgot what. Vickers often has that look just before smoke comes drifting out from under the kitchen door.

"What ho, Swashbuckler," I called as I hove into hailing distance. "Slumming?"

"Ah, Mister Boisjoly." Crocker smiled, I think, and seized my hand. "Fancy running into you here."

"Fancy that indeed, Mister Crocker," I said. "Thinking of spreading yourself thin across the clubs of the nation?"

"Herm?"

"Are you considering joining the Juniper?" I asked. "It's a topping club. I can recommend it very highly, but you should know that Carnaby, the steward, would never wear any sort of headgear indoors, least of all a fez, and while his champagne cocktail game is unparalleled, Gin Kala Khatta and Snakebite are definitely among his weaker suits."

"Oh, quite, I had no…" Crocker looked back at the Juniper as though just that moment noticing that there was a building there. "Is that a club? I mean to say, are you a member?"

"Much to the Juniper's lasting shame, I am," I confessed. "That's not to say that the Swashbucklers doesn't hold for me a child-like fascination, of course. Lunch?"

"Herm?"

"Lunch," I explained. "Mid-day refresher. Doubtless they have something comparable in the Zambezi Valley."

"Ah, lunch, yes, most generous of you, Mister Boisjoly."

It was coming up on twelve-thirty and hence late for lunch, by the standards of most members who by then were studiously snoozing over the Times crossword, and so we took the bay window table overlooking the street and next to the carvery station, the Juniper dining room equivalent of a box-seat at the Criterion.

"You do well by yourselves," declared Crocker as he peered through his eyebrows at the dining hall which is, in fact, splendid. This was just as the room had completed its convalescence from its days of Victorian purple and gilt, and was now white, clean and, in extreme contrast to the nerve centre of the Swashbucklers Society, uncluttered.

"We have a more retiring enrollment at the Juniper," I explained. "And members are discouraged from contributing to the decor. Doesn't stop them from trying, of course — Riggles Wrigley brought in an ashtray that he'd received on the occasion of his forced retirement from the Jockey Club; monstrous thing, essentially a stone plinth ornamented with brass horseheads. *And* it has hooves. Carnaby shifted it to the coat check, where it serves as a tips tray and a stark warning to us all."

"Puts me in mind of the palace at Bharatpur." Crocker nodded as he said this, as though drawing a comparison that would have been obvious to a housebound recluse.

"Never been, myself," I said, "but I've heard good

things with respect to the quality of the big game hunting on its terraces — it's where Roscoe the tiger met his end in a Homburg hat, I understand."

"Bowler, in fact," corrected Crocker, "but otherwise, bang on. Most extraordinary thing, there I was on the terrace, playing chess with the Maharani when Sir Randolph Millsip, who was in town offering me some sort of executive role at a newspaper or gas company or something he was trying to get off the ground in Jat, comes wandering in complaining that someone's nicked his bowler."

"A bowler? You're quite sure?"

"Quite sure." Crocker nodded in a manner that caused his moustache to billow, like an unfurling sail in a rippling wind, and I made a mental note to encourage him to nod again, often and vigorously. "There's old Rando, hands on hips, asking the Maharaja's wife why she's gaping at him like a ninny when she should be putting hard questions to the domestic staff. Meanwhile, behind him, is that dashed tiger, wearing the very bowler in question."

"And you say it was you that shot him?"

"No, I didn't shoot him."

"Ah, well, that tallies, then."

"Ran him through with a ceremonial shamshir."

"A sword?" I said. "What an extraordinarily unfortunate tiger. When Mister Potts shot him with the Maharajah's whist gun, he was wearing a Homburg."

"Told you that story, did he?" Crocker waved his menu at the waiter.

"I must have heard it somewhere."

"I expect he's starting to believe it himself, now, the poor nit. Carvery, I think." Crocker said this last bit to the waiter, who endorsed the decision with a sage nod.

"Same, I think," I made it unanimous, "and a bottle of tongue loosener, say, the Pommard '25."

Carvery was carved and Pommard poured and Crocker demonstrated a robust appetite. I had begun the meal with a plan to push most of the wine onto my guest by means of clever subterfuge, but in the end it proved unnecessary and indeed I was forced to pace a single glass over two thick slices of roast beef, *pommes Lyonnaises* and Yorkshire pudding, *au jus*. It was a trial.

"I take it Carnaby was no use to you," I dropped idly into the conversation as I could see the wine begin to take hold.

"Like talking to a marble mime," answered Crocker reflexively. "I mean to say, I did, indeed, have an opportunity to chat with the steward, now you mention it."

"They train them well at steward school," I explained. "Carnaby once faced down Lady Snowsill-Willit, Lady Snowsill-Willit's mother, two solicitors and a serjeant-at-arms without ever divulging whether or not Lord Snowsill-Willit was on the premises… and he wasn't. That's the sort of thing that sets your career steward apart from a chap in a fez. In any case, I trust you're satisfied now that I am indeed a member of the Juniper."

This drawing back of the veil back-footed Crocker a bit, and I stole the opportunity to mix a metaphor and play a pawn.

I knew they had been friends, though, so I selected my comments about the deceased as carefully as possible. "So, Hadley Tenpenny, rank plague rat of the first water, by all accounts, what?"

"Herm?"

"What I wonder is how he got away with it? Take that duel, where was it, the Adriatic?"

"Aegean, if we're talking about the same occasion." Crocker said this convivially, as one gently succumbing to the analgesic properties of Pommard '25.

"Possibly not," I said. "Had he cheated to win many duels on board many yachts?"

Crocker held up his fork and regarded neatly perforated layers of beef, potato, pudding, and beef again as though it held the answer. "Only the one I can think of."

"And there were no repercussions at all. Most peculiar."

"International waters, don't you know."

"Nevertheless, the other chap was English... he was English, wasn't he Mister Crocker?"

"Mmm-mm," Crocker hummed the affirmative through a mouthful. "Solicitor or something. Possibly a judge. Nothing the law could do about it, though, is there? Not like duelling is a crime or anything."

# CHAPTER FIFTEEN

# The Crisis of the Collectivist Coal Cartel

I've always felt that Scotland Yard would make an excellent gentleman's club. It's got high ceilings and high windows, many of which enjoy a smashing view of the river, and it's a labyrinth of little offices and cells and records rooms and typing rooms, any and all of which would adapt nicely to the purposes of smoking cigars, light dining, and the afternoon drift. The building is one of those two-toned brick, towered fortresses that Victorian London was always pinning onto the map of Whitehall, and its location on the Embankment is convenient to Westminster Bridge and the Abby for which it's named, the houses of parliament, Saint James, the Mall, and Steptoe and Giddy, who make my dress shirts in Covent Garden. It's also where the Metropolitan Police store its entire inventory of Ivor Wittershams.

I flatter myself to think that the garish luxury of Ivor's office was due in some small account to the aid I had provided thus far his career, for though the room was on the ground floor, were it only two stories higher and on the south wall and if it had a window, it would have a view of the Thames. As it was, though, it enjoyed a lovely perspective on a corkboard and a bank of wooden cabinets. In the middle of the room was a worn wooden desk that put me in mind of sixth form, with a tray for incoming mail on one side and outgoing mail on the other, and, in the centre, a hatbox.

"It's a pair of shoes."

"Yes, thank you Mister Boisjoly, I can see that," said Ivor, withdrawing the shoe with the bloody toe. "Does Mister Proctor not know who sent them?"

"He does not. They came by special delivery, though, so likely the post office will have some insight into the matter."

"I daresay it's evidence of something." Ivor, in the very best tradition, turned the shoe over and mulled the blood stain. "Any idea of what?"

"As actual evidence? Nothing at all. Until we know whose blood that is and, for that matter, whose shoe, it remains merely a very plucky clue. But have no doubt, Inspector, that we've made tremendous progress."

"In which direction?"

"Toward consensus," I said. "And what could be more uplifting than accord between good friends — we're finally in agreement that there's more than one crime to be solved."

"Yes, very well, Mister Boisjoly, point well made," conceded Ivor, holding up the shoe. "And we've got a bloody shoe."

"And an eye-witness."

Ivor's left eyebrow expressed surprise, while his right registered doubt. After a brief negotiation, they settled on a joint policy of courteous scepticism.

"An eye-witness? This is the first I'm hearing of it."

"It isn't, actually," I said. "According to the testimony of one A. Boisjoly the dog was barking at the same moment that the bells rang, suggesting two important things."

"Which are?"

"That the dog saw something," I said, "and that he, himself, was not the killer."

"The dog."

"Best I've got," I said. "Apart from the shoe, of course."

Ivor's eyebrows settled back into their natural state of wary corrugation and turned their attention back to the shoes.

"It would help to know who sent them to Mister Proctor, and why him, of all people."

"I should say that, at least, is obvious," I said. "The man displays an almost superhuman lack of curiosity. Absolutely legendary in our circle. As merely one example of many, Chancy once went to a wedding in Shropshire. Splashed out heavily on the gift — a Perc-o-toaster, if memory serves — and took an hotel for the weekend. Had a proper toot, by all accounts — danced with the bride and gave a reception toast that caused the groom's parents to reunite after a notoriously acrimonious ten-year separation. The whole time it never occurred to him to ask who'd invited him or why, and he only learned years later that the invitation was intended for his next-door-neighbour but one, delivered to him by accident. Their names aren't even similar. So, my guess is that whoever sent Chancy the box did so because, among all of us, he was the only one certain to not open it before its time."

"Its time?"

"Precisely, Inspector," I said. "I doubt very much that the post office will be able to tell you who sent this box, but they should be able to tell you something of far greater importance — when it was sent."

By the time I left Scotland Yard, Spring had remembered its rightful role in the daily life of the metropolis and it was discharging its responsibilities in the form of sheets of torrential rain. It's a majestic sight, London in a proper downpour — the Thames roiling and hissing, rivulets of refuse and leaves crowding and rushing down the gutters as though late for a rarely held refuse and leaf rally, citizenry splashing about with newspapers over their heads or forming jolly little mutual preservation societies beneath awnings, having been back-footed by that charming manner the spring rains have of pouncing out from behind a puffy white cloud.

I, having had the foresight to nick an umbrella from Ivor's office, made the most of the cinema of spring, and squished through Saint James Park to check on the ducks who were, predictably, ducky. Then I passed the shiny new monument to Vicky in front of the palace and lingered a bit, in case King George was clearing the downspouts and needed a hand. He wasn't — or he was round back — so I moved on to Green Park which, in the rain, is a green of which Green Park at any other time can only stand in awed jealousy. It's a deep, natural, earthy green that you can smell, and it can only be found under canopies of chestnut trees, in the rain, in the spring, in London, holding an umbrella. It's a serene, steady, timeless, otherworldly sort of green that stands in contrast to Green Park's notorious history as the venue where Edward Oxford attempted to assassinate Victoria with two empty duelling pistols and where, in 1861, William Pulteney, first Earl of Bath and John Hervey, first Earl of Bristol, in spite of their best efforts and with swords drawn, failed to make of each other the last earl of Bath and Bristol respectively.

Next was Hyde Park and the Serpentine which was overflowing its banks and looking lonesome and melancholy in exactly the way that it does not when it's reflecting the sun and supporting the weight of dozens of boaters. Hyde Park soon became Kensington Gardens which inevitably spat me out onto the sidewalk just as a taxi with the precision aim and timing for which they're widely admired dished me the depths of ditchful of vintage rainwater. I closed my umbrella and squished the remaining half a mile to number fourteen, Gloucester Gardens, and the promise of dry clothes and brandy.

໖

"Do you think we should get a cook, Vickers?" I asked as the vocative in question laid out something warm and woven.

"Is Miss Holycrook no longer giving satisfaction, sir?"

I pondered this briefly from the bedroom armchair, wrapped in thick, woolen quilt and restoring the spirit with a brandy and hot water.

"She's not, I regret to say," I admitted. "She left us in 1909. I believe she got married and moved to America from whence she has been, as a cook, remiss. You do the cooking, Vickers, and you do a bangup job of it, I was just wondering if it wasn't getting a bit overwhelming. At Wedge Hedge Square there are three houses that share one cook. Seems quite an equitable arrangement. Economical, too, if one likes jumble. Do we like jumble, Vickers?"

"The Boisjolys enjoy a more continental palate, and I fear there would be few households on Gloucester Gardens prepared to participate in such a... collective arrangement."

"I see your point, yes, a bit progressive by the silk-stocking sensibilities of Kensington."

"Precisely, sir."

"I remember when my father suggested to Elliot Lord Doncaster, who you'll recall lived next door at the time, that we pool our coal budgets and negotiate a reduction for scale," I said.

"I recall the occasion," said Vickers in a low lament. "Most regrettable."

"Questions were asked in parliament," I said. "Papa had to deny everything in a letter to the Times."

"This may have related less to a fear of Bolshevism and more to Lord Doncaster's vast holdings in the coal industry, but a most apt anecdote, nevertheless."

"Is that a fact?" I said. "And to hear him tell it, he was as much a victim as Papa."

"Lord Doncaster rarely failed to live up to his reputation as an opportunist."

"Isn't that just the sort of cross-class libel that can get you sanctioned by the League of Gentlemen's Gentlemen?"

"His Lordship's financial interests are a matter of public record, I believe."

"That's the rule, is it?" I asked. "You can say what you like, so long as someone else says it first?"

"It's more of a convention than a rule."

"Well, then, you'll be pleased to know that you're now able to speak freely of the Swashbucklers Society," I said. "I've deduced their shameful secret."

"I'm very gratified to know it, sir."

"Want to hear it? It's a corker."

"If you're referring to that which I already know, sir, then it stands to reason that I already know it."

"Fair enough," I conceded. "I confess, though, I'm still mystified how it connects to the murder of one of its more memorable members, apart from the fact that I'm sure it somehow does."

"Is this the gentleman who was found stabbed in a locked room?"

"This is one of the gentlemen who was found shot in the same locked room, two days prior. Different murder altogether," I said. "The first event was ostensibly — though manifestly not — a duel, the results of which were fiddled by an unseen hand."

"The delayed second shot," recalled Vickers.

"Just so," I confirmed. "The delayed second shot."

"More brandy?"

I examined my empty glass. "Has the weather improved?"

Vickers looked out the window. "It remains inclement."

"Umbrella inclement or ark inclement?"

"There is a decidedly biblical character to the downpour."

"Then best lay on another glass of brown muse," I said. "The problem, you see, is that in addition to both murders taking place behind locked doors, everyone involved was very concretely somewhere else at the time. In one instance the alibying witness is no less a notable than the famous London gadabout, Anthony Boisjoly himself."

"Most perplexing, sir." Vickers mixed another brandy and hot water and, instructed by that acquired telepathy exclusive to the very best valets, he added a teaspoon of honey.

"First there's fellow Juniper Lager Tenpenny, whose uncle Ratcliffe died in the aforementioned dodgy duel. Cheers," I said, receiving the snifter. "He's the first to admit that he hopes that it was his uncle who died thoroughly and well and last, making Lager the sole heir to the tontine. But he was at home at number one, Wedge Hedge Square, as witnessed by the maid, Miss Belsize."

"Is Miss Belsize a reliable witness?"

"Not in the slightest," I said, "but she has no reason to lie, in this case, and at any rate even Vicks says that Lager arrived at the scene after she did."

"Vicks?"

"Victoria Tenpenny," I explained. "The other heir in question, this time via the circuitous route of her uncle Hadley, the second duelist. Having said that, both Vicks and Lager assert that the other is, for various reasons, not qualified to collect on the inheritance — Vicks says that Ratcliffe Tenpenny was no Tenpenny at all, and Lager contends that Hadley left a trail of tiny Tenpennys wherever he went, and he went everywhere, meaning that somewhere out there is at least one person with a better claim to the tontine than Vicks, who holds the mere rank of niece."

The storm changed course at this point and what had been an undisciplined deluge was given direction by a willful wind that had taken a consuming interest in my bedroom window. The drumming distracted Vickers, who regarded the window with composed censure.

"Best pour yourself one of these, Vickers," I said, looking at him in parallax through my snifter. "It's the only accompaniment to a thorny story on a stormy afternoon."

The air in the bedroom became a jolly mix of cool mist and warm brandy. Vickers stood by the window and kept an eye on the storm and held his drink as one musing on the meaning of it all.

"I've looked into both claims," I continued, "and both are, at best, twaddle. Ratcliffe Tenpenny was indeed illegitimate for the first part of his life, which he spent in seclusion in the remote village of Gutter Folly, but even if that excluded him by law from inheriting, which it does not, he was legally recognised by his father in his twenty-first year. As for the speculative offspring of Hadley Tenpenny, one would suppose that if any such claimants exist they'd have spoken up long before now."

"It must be a comfort to the heirs to have their claims confirmed, at the very least."

"Not much, no, because it means that unless it's determined which man died first, the crown will claim the wealth of the tontine. Indeed, the investigation of the counterclaims may have only muddied the waters further," I said. "The Boy's Own Tales that is the life of Hadley Tenpenny has it that he nobbled the competition in a duel held at sea and for the honour of an unnamed woman, and a girl of the unlikely name of Quiescence is introduced as a peripherally interested party who, as we speak, is lamenting an unprecedented period of stability in the price of an ounce of gold."

"How capricious young ladies are," deplored Vickers, shaking his head sadly over his brandy. "In my day it was feather pelisses. Every girl had to have one." He looked up at me with lucid recall. "Two if they attended the opera with any frequency."

"Well, Quiescence, popularly known as Quip, has a particular interest in the unshakeable value of gold — twenty-four ounces worth, give or take, set aside for her grandmother by Terrence Tenpenny some forty-odd years ago. She affects surprise at having received the consideration, but it could well be that she felt entitled to more."

"Would Mister Tenpenny not have been better counselled to put the money into some sort of interest-bearing instrument?"

"Mister Tenpenny would have been better counselled to put the money in a sock," I said. "But he was counselled by none other than the grandfather of Chauncy the Chancy Lawyer, who carried on the proud family tradition of consistently choosing the third of two good choices. Talking of Chancy, he turns out to be a dark horse — he's got a first from Cambridge."

"The university?"

"That's exactly what I asked," I said. "Yes, a first from Cambridge University. Not, unsurprisingly, in law, but it does put a different spin on the chap — might he be hiding something in addition to academic excellence?"

The storm insinuated itself into the room, now, in that earthy, fresh, vaporous way heavy weather has of penetrating closed windows and thick walls. Vickers bent and performed arcane rites of spring with the gas fireplace, and in a moment the room was a warm sanctuary against the raging elements.

"They do electric heating at Wedge Hedge Square," I said. "Or at least, they do when it's not too damp, which is rather when it's needed most I'd have thought. Apparently the cellar assumes the slightest pretext to flood to the rafters."

"That sounds a most impractical arrangement." Vickers said this distractedly while, in a fit of inspired genius, placing our hot water pot on the little furnace.

"Well, that's the price of progress," I said. "It's like when we got the telephone laid on — I've never once been home when it's rung, but when's the last time I missed a telegram?"

"A keen observation, if I may say so, sir."

"You may, Vickers, and keep it coming. We have thick skins, we Boisjolys." I drained my glass and returned it to the shop for refitting. "That leaves us with Kimberly Brickstock, who also had a strong alibi for the first murder and an absolutely airtight one for the second."

"It was Mister Brickstock who was dispatched with a knife, if memory serves."

"Memory does serve, Vickers, like a third-generation valet." The simile manifested in a newly heated snifter of brandy. "But, prior to being cooled to room temperature, Brickstock was Vicks Tenpenny's alibi — he was with her when the shots were heard — the starting pistol, if you will, to this perplexing mystery."

"Would Mister Brickstock have otherwise figured among your suspects?"

"Not very prominently, no," I said. "His was an intelligence which could be charitably described as unpretentious, but he did ostensibly have cause to wish ill upon Hadley Tenpenny, who apparently objected to

Brickstock's romantic overtures toward Vicks. Thought he was a 'fat idler', in the words of the deceased. By all accounts he was a plain speaker, though, with a low tolerance for indolence, and to be fair Brickstock was more of the immovable object than the unstoppable force, if you take my meaning."

"I do, indeed."

"Nevertheless, Brickstock got it into his head that he had some insight into the crime, and he let it be known that he meant to share this brainswell with Inspector Wittersham," I continued. "Two days later, he was heard exchanging angry words with an unidentified woman. The following day he's summoned back to Wedge Hedge Square where he's perforated beyond all hope of repair."

"And had he occasion to share his derivations with the inspector?"

"He had not, sadly," I said. "Although a clue, to something, was left in his name — a pair of shoes were mailed to him care of Chancy's office — quite smart, too — Cuban heels, braided strap, tooled leather in pastel browns, tasteful little hint of blood on the right toe..."

"A most vexing confluence of circumstance," sympathised Vickers.

"The *mot juste,* Vickers," I agreed. "Everybody with an interest in the tontine is either dead or couldn't possibly have committed either murder."

"Forgive me for pointing it out, sir, but you've neglected to account for Elliot Lord Doncaster, whom I believe you mentioned as material to the case."

"Different case, actually, Vickers. Different conversation entirely, in fact. Lord Doncaster was the villain in the tale of my father's ill-fated venture into the perilous underworld of coal delivery. It was His Lordship who secretly benefited from scuppering Papa's syndicate."

"Of course, forgive me, sir."

I never got around to forgiving Vickers, because something I'd just said about Lord Doncaster was lingering still, hanging about and affecting to look for his gloves but clearly hoping to have a quiet word about something important. And then, in a flash, I knew exactly what his lordship wanted to tell me.

"Vickers, take a cable, will you?"

"Certainly, sir." He withdrew his telegraph pad and pencil.

"To Inspector Wittersham, Scotland etc... Please round up all concerned parties and meet me at Wedge Hedge Square, seven-ish... Most urgent... Anty... PS including the dog." I leapt from my thinking chair and threw off my thinking quilt and reached for my action trousers. "Send that, and then order me a taxi, or, if you see fit, a gondola. I'm going to Wedge Hedge Square."

"So I gather, sir," said Vickers. "I expect the inspector will be more compliant with your wishes if he understood your reasoning."

"Always the stickler for protocol, Vickers," I said. "Very well, add the following... Have solved the case of the Tenpenny tontine."

# CHAPTER SIXTEEN

# The Wisdom of the Waterproof Wittersham

I've never met a man as watertight as Ivor Wittersham — submarines and jam jars, possibly, but never a man quite so prepared to face London in the spring. There I was, at the gate to Wedge Hedge Square, under a spindly umbrella which might have been made of fish net for all the protection it offered against the rain which whirled about and came at one from all directions at once, when the inspector issued from the cascade like Aphrodite emerging from the foam. He carried a golf umbrella like an oil-cloth basilica and he was otherwise swaddled to Wittersham code in trench coat, galoshes, broad-brimmed fedora and the smug, 'fine-weather-we're-having-what?' insouciance of the over-equipped.

"Is that my umbrella?" he asked.

"As an officer of the law, Inspector, I would have assumed that you'd know that all umbrellas, without exception, are community property, like the rain itself. You don't hear me asking if that's my puddle you're standing in."

We both of us looked down, then, at the water rushing at us from both ends of the street to overflow the runoff grates where the road dipped to accommodate Wedge Hedge Square. The waters were rapidly rising.

"Constable… There will be a constable waiting for us at number fifty-seven," said Ivor.

"To which constable do you refer, Inspector?"

"The same one who was here yesterday morning."

"Ah, quite, that would be Constable…"

"Correct."

"Correct what? You never introduced us."

Ivor looked to the skies in support for some as-yet-unnamed, distasteful duty before him. "His name is Penleigh Constable."

Briefly, I could only smile my joy. "His name is Constable Pen Constable?"

"Now you know why I didn't introduce you."

"Of course," I said. "You were probably saving it for my birthday. This is the most delightful thing I've heard since learning that Queen Mary can't help giggling at the sight of Beefeaters."

"Well, now you know this, too," said Ivor with what I thought a dismissive attitude toward my Beefeater scoop. "I sent the constable on ahead to gather your audience."

"Suspects," I gently corrected.

"I know what I said."

We pushed through the wringing jungle and into Wedge Hedge Square where, silhouetted in the downpour like a monument to silent despair, was Constable Constable. Rain streamed from his helmet and his uniform was soaked and swollen so that the poor chap resembled a Yorkshire pudding forgotten in a gravy boat overnight.

"You were alright to wait inside, Constable," said Ivor.

"Yes, sir, thank you sir," sputtered the constable. "I'm afraid that I have yet to gather all parties, as instructed, sir."

"Who's missing?"

"The dog, sir. Scottish Terrier named…" Constable Pen Constable withdrew his notebook and looked sadly at the mass of smeared and soggy pages, "…Ludovic, I think, sir."

"You haven't been able to find our man Lucifer?" I asked. "Just stand where you are, Constable, he'll find you. I can't imagine anything that dog would find more irresistible than a policeman in uniform."

"This is what I was doing, sir," explained Constable Constable, "on the advice of Miss Tenpenny. She told me to go stand in the rain and the dog would be by soon enough."

"She's funny that way, is our Vicks."

"Yes, sir. Most amusing."

"Is this dog absolutely crucial to your big reveal, Mister Boisjoly?" asked Ivor.

"Vital," I said. "I rely on him for moral support, if nothing else."

"He's probably just staying out of the rain."

"With not one but two police officers in the square?" I scoffed. "Standing on the road, I might add, in open contempt of oft-stated policy? You grossly underestimate the animal's sense of duty."

"Very well." Ivor returned his attention to Constable Pen Constable. "Is everyone gathered at number fifty-seven? Have you asked them all if they'd seen the dog?"

"Yes, sir. None of them reported sighting the animal."

"Just a tick," I said. "You brought everyone to number fifty-seven and left them there while you looked for Lucifer?"

"Well, no, not as such, sir," said Constable Constable. "I asked them to be at number fifty-seven by seven o'clock."

"And told them all that you were looking for the dog."

"The inspector said that he was an important eye-witness," said the constable, with the tone of one endeavouring to fairly distribute blame.

"Inspector," I said. "I have reason to believe that if we don't act with haste, there will shortly be a third victim, if it's not already too late."

"Who? The dog?"

"Exactly."

"Mister Boisjoly, this is a murder inquiry," said Ivor in that weary tone he employs when restating the obvious, which he does rather a lot. "You can't expect us to give priority to some stray."

"Hardly some stray, Inspector. He's key to the solution and, in many regards, a colleague. You can't very well desert a colleague," I said. "And I don't want to embarrass you, Inspector, but you should know that he had some very flattering things to say about you, both professionally and personally."

Ivor glared at me in the darkness and rain and then, preceded by a little incredulous shake of the head, he said, "Constable, institute a house-to-house search for the dog. I'll manage number fifty-seven."

"Sir," said Constable Constable and splashed off toward number one. Ivor and I set sail for number fifty-seven.

There's a tone — or perhaps frequency is the word I want — to the din produced by a room full of people who dislike one another's company. It's not unlike the sound that an orchestra makes when tuning up before a poorly-rehearsed musical, only less harmonious.

The salon of number fifty-seven was tuning up nicely — Vicks and Lager were exchanging a brisk bagatelle, Babbage sat in an armchair, moaning a monody to himself, Chancy was chirping some light air to Quip who hummed a tuneful reply, Miss Belsize was buffetting a basso buffo of her own invention. As one does in these environments, everyone raised the volume because everyone else had raised the volume. All the piece wanted, I felt, was the crescendo, what they call the Big Finish in broadway circles, and I was about to beat a makeshift gong composed of the drinks tray and the drinks when the lights flickered.

Silence followed, as it invariably does flickering lights, and I seized the moment.

"Good evening where's the dog?"

"The dog?" asked Lager. "What about the dog? That constable was going on about Lucifer, too, what do you want with the dog?"

"Never mind what I want with the dog, Lager old man, just tell me when it was you last saw him, and where."

Helpless glances and deep, meaningful shrugs were freely exchanged.

"I certainly didn't see him," said Chancy. "Or I'd be in a tree."

"Probably digging up the garden," suggested Vicks

with, in my view of the gravity of the situation, a disinterested air.

Variations of this attitude were expressed in sequence until I held up an authoritative 'that will do' hand.

"One of you knows exactly where Lucifer is," I said. "I'm prepared to show leniency in exchange for a frank and full admission."

At that moment the lights again had a fit of indecision and in that same flash I knew where Lucifer was, and that his time was running out.

"This way Inspector," I said, leading into the hall and to the stairwell entrance. We regrouped on the landing before the elevator. "Listen…"

"I don't hear anything," said Ivor.

"No, you wouldn't," I said, cocking my head toward the stairs. "You don't have the connection to Lucifer that I have."

"I'll say."

"He's in the cellar." I dashed down the stairs to the door, under which water was already flowing. The door was like a solid thing, as though it had been painted onto a stone wall.

"Help me Inspector," I called, and Ivor and I threw our combined weight against the vault.

"It's no good," he said. "It's swollen with damp. Probably hasn't been opened in years — at least it means you're wrong about the dog being in there."

"But I'm not, Inspector." I ran back up the stairs. "The lift goes to the cellar."

Ivor and I threw our coats to the floor and pushed into the iron cage. I pressed the cellar button repeatedly until the clunking and grinding announced our slow descent into the depths.

"It would have been quicker to dig," observed Ivor.

"It's the only way, I fear," I said but then put a finger to my lips — as we drew deeper underground and the sound of the gears faded above us the distant, desperate yelps of a Scottish Terrier out of his element became clear to both of us.

"I hear him," said Ivor.

And then the lights went out, and the lift stopped.

"Oh, well, pox," I said.

"Hang on," said Ivor from somewhere in the void. I heard him fumble, swear, fumble some more, then a brief pause, and then a slight, subtle squeak. "There's a hand crank."

The crank screeched and Ivor grunted and ever so gradually we descended. At least, in retrospect I know that we descended, but in the dark and at a velocity that made the lift seem in its better days dangerously quick, we might have been moving sideways for all I could tell. Our disposition became clearer in time as our feet became submerged and then, after what seemed an interminable period, our knees.

"Are we there yet?" asked Ivor.

I tried to open the gate. "No," I said. "Bit further I expect."

The agonisingly slow pace continued to count down in the blackness in laborious, regular, clunks.

Finally Ivor could crank no further.

"We must be on the bottom," he said. "Listen…"

"Oh, dear Lord."

There was only the sound of rushing water. The rain was pouring into the cellar from all over Pimlico, and the level was to our hips, now — well above the maximum elevation of a fully grown terrier's snout.

"We're too late," said Ivor. "Sorry, Boisjoly."

I listened still. The currents and eddies wooshed and hushed in a fixed, consistent rhythm, like something settled, something done, and this is the way it would always be.

"It's my own, Chancy-witted fault," I said. "Too clever by half is never clever enough, is it? I had to say that Lucifer was an eye-witness."

I'd never really known until then the leaden-hearted feeling of letting down a friend. I'd done bad turns accidentally and, candidly, as often as not deliberately, but until that moment I hadn't known what it was to trade a life for a flippant remark.

"You worked out he was down here," said Ivor in some clumsy clutch at comfort. Then he splashed and struggled in the darkness. "How do you get a dog like that into a cellar, anyway?" I heard the lift gate open and Ivor must have waded out. Next there was a fumbling and a folding and then, extraordinarily, a match striking, and then there was light.

I could see only Ivor as he withdrew his official police notebook and, even more extraordinarily, set it on fire.

"How is that possibly dry?" I asked.

"I'm always prepared for weather," said Ivor, as his notebook-torch spread orange light across the little triangular, subterranean lake that had formed beneath Wedge Hedge Square. The flame reflected and rippled on the water toward the centre of the cellar where the boiler stood like a rusty, cubic island. On top of the island was

Lucifer the Scottish Terrier, with a leg of lamb in his mouth.

"That's how you get a dog like that into a cellar," concluded Ivor. "And that's why he stopped barking — he was saving his leg of lamb from the rising waters."

Lucifer danced that nervous, frustrated dance of a dog clearly craving the power of speech. He simpered a little soprano through clenched teeth and clattered toward me as I reached out for him.

"One of us smells like a wet dog," said Ivor as he closed us into the lift and discarded his torch. He slowly cranked us back to the surface. "I think it's you."

# CHAPTER SEVENTEEN

# The Glaring Bearing of the Unerring Herring

"What ho, wary gallery of likely suspects," I said as we returned to the salon. I released Lucifer and, after pausing for a shivering distribution of cellar water in all directions, he withdrew to a corner to have a discreet word with his leg of lamb.

Countless candles had been laid on in our absence, and the room looked like the scene of a vigil for a well-regarded pope. Constable Constable had joined the party and he was the only one — apart from the deserving Inspector Wittersham and myself — without a drink. Instead, he stood at the door, shivering. Lager had worked up a very respectable flame in a chafing dish and Ivor and I gathered around it.

"We could stand a couple of rugs, if there are any on hand…" I spoke this into the void but all eyes turned to Miss Belsize, who snapped into action with a quick "Wasn't me doesn't have sense to come in out of the rain."

"Go with her, Constable," said Ivor, putting an end to debate, and Miss Belsize and the constable, quibbling and dribbling respectively, disappeared into the darkness.

Lager stepped up to his hosting duties with the surprisingly resourceful strategy of balancing the entire decanter of brandy over the chafing flame.

"Couple of warm ones, gentlemen? Looks as though you've earned it. Got the dog back all right, I see."

"He was in the cellar," I said.

"I knew he was clever." Lager glanced at the dog who met his eye with a vigilant regard for his leg of lamb. "How did he use the lift?"

"He had assistance."

"Anyway, all's well and all that, what?" Lager poured two cosy snifters. "Go on Inspector, I daresay you need one, and you must be off-duty by now."

"I'm never off-duty," said Ivor, but he received the brandy and brought it to his nose for a deep, restorative inhale. He shot me a conspiratorial eye and then heaved a good half-ounce of brandy into the internal combustion inspector.

"I understand you've got it all sorted, Anty," enthused Lager. "I knew he would, you know," he said to Ivor. "It was me who asked him to look in, you know."

"All done but the wailing from the visitors' gallery," I assured him. In the same moment Miss Belsize returned with thick blankets and a swaddling constable, and Ivor and I wrapped ourselves against the cold air and colder stares. The storm hummed and thrummed outside and a sheet of wind slapped the window like a sloppy great hand. The candlelight danced in the crossed currents of an unheated room in an old house on a stormy night. Vicks, Babbage, Belsize, Lager, Chancy, and Quip regarded one another with furtive, speculative glances, and then regarded me with hope and expectation which, in the poor light, rather resembled foot-tapping impatience.

"Let us review the evidence." My proposal was met with a collective moan, much like those which in boyhood I would orchestrate in reply to 'Let us review the fourth declension.'

"But Anty, you do *know* who died second, don't you?" asked Lager.

"Of course I do."

"Well?"

"Very well, indeed, Lager. I'm certain of it, in fact," I said. "But what everyone wants to know, of course, is why."

"No, I think everyone wants to know who died second."

"Really? Everyone? Vicks?"

Vicks nodded gravely and this had a rather leader-of-the-pack effect on Miss Belsize and Chancy, who also expressed a preference for the abridged version.

"Well, that's modern audiences for you," I lamented. "Good job you lot weren't representative of the ticket-buying public in Shakespeare's day, or Hamlet would have just ended with 'oh, well, I guess it's just not to be, then.' What are your thoughts Inspector? You really are the voice of authority."

"If you can manage to get to the point without too many of your anecdotes," said Ivor, wearily and warily.

"A promise as easily kept as made," I said. "For we both know there's no such thing as too many of my anecdotes. Let us begin, then, with a quick census of the principal players — Ratcliffe and Hadley Tenpenny ostensibly shot each other in the drawing-room of this very house, four days ago, as the unexpected consequence of a novel approach to settling who should inherit the immense wealth of the Tenpenny Tontine. We know that's not what happened, though, so we look to a third party — someone else who would benefit from the death of one or perhaps both men."

"Both?" It was Vicks who said this, I think, but there appeared to be a general clamour to point out the anomaly.

"Could be," I said. "We've all assumed that the motive was the tontine and, I have it on good authority, it's a jolly sizable motive — so sizable, in fact, that it may be eclipsing the real one."

"Such as?" asked Lager.

"Revenge?" I took in Quip from the corner of my eye, and noted that she affected to be distracted by the tradecraft which Lucifer was practising on his leg of lamb. "Ratcliffe Coleridge was made a Tenpenny and snatched away from Drab House in his twenty-first year, after which the fortunes of the house and the town into which it sinks went from worse to worst."

Quip looked up from her study of the dog's craftsmanship. "Yes, I noticed that myself, Anty..." she confessed. "In fact, I noticed it when you brought it to my attention."

"So you say," I said. "But you do have something of an inside track with the parish clerk's office. And it's a small town."

"Half of the population of which are called Coleridge," she pointed out. "I didn't even know there was any money until Chauncy sent my nan that cable. And even then it's turned out to be a hundred quid. You think I killed two men I'd never heard of, in a town I never visit, for a hundred pounds?"

This otherwise flawless woman's baffling bias against London still rankled — I moved swiftly along to spare us both further sorrow.

"Talking of Chancy, he does seem to play a curiously central role in this affair."

Chancy recognised his own name in the proceedings, and little else.

"Oh, rather," he said.

"Rather what, Chancy?" I asked.

"Just, rather. I mean to say, quite. What?"

"Is it true that you have a first from Cambridge, Chancy?" I asked.

"No," he said, with a self-deprecating snort. "Double first."

"Architectural engineering and philosophy," I said. "And yet you didn't work out that the crown of the arch was, literally, the crown of the arch."

"Seems rather obvious, now, doesn't it?" Chancy smiled sheepishly at Quip. "I'm easily distracted."

"And yet you're a solicitor, obliged to take on the family practice when your father died suddenly."

"Yes, poor chap." Chancy gazed nostalgically into his brandy. "He was always doing things like that — falling down embankments and dying suddenly. I mean, he only did that last bit the one time, but he was forever falling down embankments in the interim."

"About the same time, according to Hadley Tenpenny's own carefully curated legend, he killed a man in a duel, after being found in a compromising lower-deck with the chap's wife." I gauged Chancy's reaction to this, which was vacant as an inflated balloon. "I understand that Hadley openly admitted — the cynical amongst Tenpenny connoisseurs might say bragged — that his victory on that occasion was largely thanks to the precaution of nobbling his opponent's weapon."

"I say," protested Lager. "Dashed unsporting, that."

"Something of a theme at the Swashbucklers Society," I said, adding for the benefit of late arrivals, "His club, you understand. Not a man among them who can't tell you at least a dozen stories about the time he talked his way out of a noose or ran a blade through an unarmed tiger on a terrace."

"Are tigers *ever* armed?" asked Ivor, more as a point of order than a real interest in feline zoology.

"Not famously, no, but they don't often wear bowler hats, either," I said. "These Swashbuckler chaps are indiscriminate predators. All in a day's work, I suppose, when your leisure time reads like something Kipling scribbled on the back of an envelope while waiting for the four-thirty-seven from Rangoon, but Hadley Tenpenny took the philosophy in bold new directions with scores of illegitimate children from Wagga Wagga to Waterloo. And yet, none of them have spoken up, for reasons which will shortly become evident."

"It doesn't matter why — I'm Uncle Hadley's only known heir," said Vicks.

"Hang on," said Ivor. "Bowler hats?"

"Or Homburgs," I conceded. "The question is mired in controversy. However Vicks is correct, for the moment, that she's Hadley Tenpenny's only known heir, which brings us to Kimberly Brickstock."

"What's he got to do with it?" asked Vicks.

"Well, I mean to say, he's one of the victims," I pointed

out, rather surprised that I had to.

"I mean, what's he got to do with my inheritance?"

"He knew what it was worth," I explained. "His family managed many of the assets of the tontine — he was probably the only one among you who had some idea of its value."

"And?"

"I met Mister Brickstock and, as a romantic, he put me in mind of an adult turbot whose acquaintance I once made during a fishing holiday in the Irish Sea," I said. "I expect that the tontine was the fiery heart of his incandescent affection for you. No offence, doubtless he also thought highly of your ready hand with the sticky bun."

"Be that as it may," Vicks shrugged and drew theatrically on her brandy. "He had no way of knowing which of us would inherit."

"You knew him better than I did, but during our brief acquaintance I found Mister Brickstock to have a disarmingly wholesale overestimation of his own intelligence — he may have had what he thought was a plan. Furthermore, we know he had solid cause to believe that it was Uncle Hadley who stood between him and happiness, and not your reticence to marry a chap I've heard you describe — affectionately, I'm sure — as a dim, desperate dollop."

"If you've got something to say, I wish you'd just say it," said Vicks.

"You'd be astounded how often I hear that."

"I'll bet I wouldn't."

"No, probably not," I agreed. "But as our friendship grows closer you'll come to delight in my eccentricities.

However, that does bring us, as scheduled, to the argument Mister Brickstock was heard to have had with an unidentified combattant whom our witnesses, Chancy and Lager, could only determine was neither Chancy nor Lager but a woman, or someone who sounded uncannily like one."

"Weren't me," said Miss Belsize, reflexively.

"I didn't say it was," I countered.

"You was about to."

"That's true," I acknowledged. "I was. Miss Tenpenny makes the same claim, and I can add with almost complete conviction that one of you is telling the truth. The other is fully aware that it was at this moment that Mister Brickstock put his ploy in motion."

"Ploy?" said Lager, dubiously.

"For lack of a better word," I said. "No, wait, gambit. His clever gambit."

"What clever gambit?" asked Vicks with a mirthless laugh contrived to suggest that Burly Brickstock wouldn't have known a clever gambit if he was sat next to one on a Ferris wheel.

"The clever gambit," I announced, "that cost Mister Brickstock his life."

An entertaining course of sidelong squints o'erleapt each other as Lager, Chancy, Belsize, Vicks, and Quip all tried to catch the others' reactions without betraying one of their own. The protracted volley was finally broken by a scratch and a sparkly little explosion as Ivor lit a match and put it to his pipe.

I seized the moment. "Mister Brickstock was blackmailing Victoria Tenpenny into agreeing to marry him."

"What? How?" scoffed Lager.

"He threatened to reveal proof that she had committed murder."

"Absurd," adjudged Lager.

"Is it?" I asked. "You said yourself that she was as much in need of the oofum as anyone, and it might be argued that her situation was more dire — if Victoria Tenpenny didn't come into her little own — and be right skippy about it — then she'd be left with no option better than lawfully wedded perpetuity to the broadening Brickstock panorama across the breakfast table."

Vicks stood stiff and stark against the mantelpiece, as though formed of the same cold, belligerent marble. Her arms were crossed tightly before her and she dangled her snifter in her hand. The candlelight danced on damp pools in her eyes as she gazed at the storm.

"It's true," she said.

"Steady on, Vicks." Lager laughed this line, the way one does when one is trying to gain popular support. "You didn't kill anyone." Lager addressed an aside to Ivor, "She didn't kill anyone." And then turned to me. "What sort of proof, anyway?"

"What the French call *un héring rouge.*"

"A red earring?"

"Herring," I said. "This entire mystery has been awash with the things — great sholes of red herrings, distracting from the simple truth of what actually happened, starting with a bloody shoe."

"Language, old man."

"No, I mean an actual shoe with literal blood on it," I said. "A blood-red herring that takes its place alongside the pool of blood in which Kimberly Brickstock died, a smudge on the floor of the reading room and another on the shirt of one of the victims."

"All red herrings?" asked Lager.

"Positively crimson," I said. "Along with Hadley Tenpenny's duel in the Aegean Sea, feigned handicap, vast collection of bizarre memorabilia, and illegitimate children. As for Ratcliffe Tenpenny, he provides his own distractions in the form of an altered birth certificate, a baptismal certificate and the suspicious absence of a vaccination certificate."

"Say, that's right," said Quip. "There wasn't one."

"Made mandatory, I believe you said, in 1853," I noted. "Which brings us to the actually-quite-obvious hiding place of the tontine deed which produced further fishy business of its own in the form of separate legacies for Ratcliffe, Hadley, and Willow Willoughby."

"What's that? A separate legacy?" Lager addressed Chancy, who had been watching the candlelight play on the ceiling. "Is this true, Chancy? Are there separate bequests? For how much?"

"A hundred pounds," answered Quip on Chancy's behalf. "Converted to gold by Chancy's grandfather."

"Blimey," mused Lager. "That must be worth... I don't know, five thousand, at the very least."

"A hundred pounds," answered Quip, again adding, with trenchant admiration, "Gold has really held its price."

"Of course," said Lager with resigned forbearance. "What's all this got to do with who died second, Anty?"

"I see now that I ought to have defined my terms before setting out," I said. "The expression 'red herring' derives

213

from the practice of dragging a pickled herring across the path of a hunting dog in training, to engender that steely-eyed focus that sets your honed hound of the chase apart from a beagle that just likes running around in fields, barking at things."

"Not sure I follow, old man."

"The legacies have nothing to do with who died second. That's the whole point of a red herring," I said. "Neither does the note delivered to Mister Brickstock at Claridge's, the unnecessary wheelchairs, the pictures on Ratcliffe's mantelpiece and the invisible letters that Quip's grandmother continues to write to long-dead correspondents."

"What's this about them wheelchairs?" demanded Miss Belsize. "I carried meals up those rickety stairs three times a day every day for five years — are you telling me now those two idlers could walk?"

"Until quite recently Hadley Tenpenny was a major attraction at his club, where he traded tales with experts in the salon — one narrow flight of stairs above Lombard Street," I said. "But that was just a bit of mischief, part of the light-hearted one-upmanship that doubtless made life at number fifty-seven, Wedge Hedge Square, one long hoot, and certainly in keeping with the spirit of the Swashbucklers Society."

"I don't see how," said Lager. "It's an adventurers club."

"Portuguese Man O'War don't hunt in packs, Lager," I pointed out, "there's no such thing as a blubber gun, skeet shooting was invented twenty years after Hadley's fantasy encounter in the Aegean Sea where, he would have had us believe, he'd gone with a crew of Frenchmen hunting a creature from Greek Mythology. The doorman at his club is a stuffed tiger in a bowler hat that every member has killed at least once. The Swashbucklers Society is not an adventurers club — it's a liars club."

"That... swaggering... blustering... blathering... posing... pretentious..." Vicks was building up an impressive head of steam — like an old locomotive climbing a hill it had always disliked — I felt sure that I would have to censor the destination when I recounted the evening to Vickers, "...windbag! It was all made-up? He never taught William McKinley to build an igloo?"

"He did not."

"He didn't stand in for Lord Curzon when Czar Nicholas challenged him to a blindfolded fencing match?"

"Unequivocally not. There was no such event."

"Didn't write Gunga Din?"

"You're not telling me you believed that."

"He could be very convincing," said Lager. "It was in the telling, I think. So... I don't know…"

"Casually fraudulent?" I suggested. "I know. I've observed the phenomenon under the cold, white light of the Juniper, where no man can lie for long, and I can assure you that it was all the slosh and slurry of the red herring in its natural habitat."

"Then, Vicks didn't kill Hadley," Lager somehow concluded from all that.

"Of course not, Lager old Juniper," I said. "Hadley Tenpenny was killed by your uncle, Ratcliffe Tenpenny, who in turn was murdered by the only person who could possibly have done it — you."

# CHAPTER EIGHTEEN

# Pitiful Plan, Performed Poorly

"There was a time back in '14, I think it was, when my father was struck by an ill-fated inspiration to form a coal-buying syndicate with our immediate neighbors in Kensington..." I began.

"Please, Mister Boisjoly," said Ivor, withering and shivering over his brandy. "Is this absolutely necessary?"

"Is art necessary, Inspector?" I countered. "Or Bearnaise sauce or children's laughter or good friends who'll set their valuables alight in aid of saving the life of a terrier with whom they've only ever been on distant terms?"

"Could you not just explain how it was done?"

"Forgive the inspector's impatience," I explained to the avid spectators. "He heard most of this in the lift."

"It was interminable." Ivor shook his head and softened the hard memory with another draw of his brandy.

"Indeed," I concurred. "That contrivance is agonisingly slow."

"Yes," said Ivor. "That too."

"Do any of you know Elliot Lord Doncaster?" I asked. "You'd recall meeting him, looks just like Baron Parmoor, who in turn bears an uncanny resemblance to a hopelessly diseased elm in an ermine cape. Displays an energetic cunning in the pilfering of snuff and ducking out before his round. No? Well, no matter. It would add colour, of course, to have a sketch of the man's character, but it's enough to know that he was our immediate neighbor in my father's day and affected delirious support for the coal syndicate."

Lager waved his hand weakly. "Quick aside, if you will, Anty."

"Doubtless you're anxious to return to the question of guilt," I sympathised. "In a moment, Lager. You see, while Lord Doncaster was drinking my father's whisky and subscribing to his plan to reduce our mutual heating burden, someone was putting it about the better circles that Papa was a dangerous radical, endorsing everything from price controls on coal and bread to abolition of the monarchy."

"I'm sorry, Boisjoly, but this seems very much a departure from the point," said Ivor.

"Exactly, Inspector," I said, for I believe in encouraging audience participation. "I recently learned from my man, Vickers, that the source of the rumours was none other than Elliot Lord Doncaster himself who, I'll remind you for dramatic effect, was casting himself as a fellow victim. It was rather a watershed moment for me, for a number of reasons."

"I see it now," claimed Lager, dubiously. "This is, what do you call it, your process, right Anty?"

"It is," I confirmed. "Probably the key part — certainly the most theatrical — it's when I reveal the killer. It's also where I show the inspector, who had his doubts, that the Boisjoly code transcends loyalty to friends."

"I concede the point," said Ivor handsomely, and we touched our snifters together and drank to higher ideals.

"You're not serious, Anty old man," said Lager weakly.

"Very, very rarely," I confessed. "However, if you're wondering if I can prove that you killed not only your uncle but Kimberly Brickstock then you may set your mind to rest — I can."

"Are you going to tell us how he did it?" asked Quip.

"As mentioned and as is so often the case, it was deceptively simple," I said. "Both locked-room murders — that of Ratcliffe Tenpenny and Kimberly Brickstock — didn't occur in locked rooms."

"Of course they did," insisted Lager. "You were there, Vicks. Tell him."

"She was there, exactly as she was supposed to be," I agreed. "And she saw what she was supposed to see — two men, having shot each other, motionless and bloody. But Ratcliffe Tenpenny was still alive. He'd nobbled the competition, probably by loading his own weapon the night before, and had shot Hadley before the festivities commenced. Then he fired the other pistol and used some of his victim's blood to set the scene; he dobbed a bit on his own shirt and then — and this is the bit that you probably thought was tremendously clever — he wrote something on the floor in blood, so there'd be no question that it was he who had died second."

"Nonsense," adjudged Babbage, whom I had assumed had fallen asleep. "They both would have died instantly, and there was nothing written on the floor."

"These were the inevitable flaws in the execution that, had Ratcliffe and Lager reflected on their plan, they might have foreseen — they hadn't realised that a bullet through the heart would preclude the possibility of a second shot, and they didn't count on Victoria Tenpenny, on seeing the message on the floor — doubtless something short but meaningful, such as, 'I win' — would step on it, leaving a blood stain on her shoe."

"I swear, Boisjoly, I've known blunt instruments with greater powers of concentration. I've told you — and I expect I'll be telling you twice more before the night is over — I examined both men and they were fully and decisively deceased," insisted Babbage. Then he addressed Ivor. "Young people. I blame the talking pictures." Ivor nodded sagely.

"They were indeed dead by the time you examined them," I agreed. "But Ratcliffe Tenpenny wasn't shot — he was stabbed."

"Stabbed?"

"Through the heart," I said. "With the tapered ramrod of his pistol. After the discovery of the bodies, Victoria saw Mister Brickstock to the gate, and Miss Belsize took a strategic nap. For a brief but consequential moment, one person was left alone with Ratcliffe Tenpenny while he still lived — Lager Tenpenny."

"What an absurd theory," laughed Lager. "You're suggesting that my uncle willingly cooperated in a plot that required him to be stabbed to death? Anyone who knew him will tell you how ridiculous that is."

"Not willingly, no," I said. "He thought that he was going to survive the ordeal — the plan was that Mister Babbage would pronounce him dead, and he would assume an impenetrable disguise…"

"I would never do anything of the sort," alleged Babbage.

"Quite sure?" I asked. "Mister Tenpenny offered to buy your plot of land, did he not? Freeing you to mangle all the wurzels you could lay hands on…"

"Nothing wrong with that," asserted Babbage.

"Nothing at all, provided one is not a wurzel nor related to one by blood," I agreed. "But Lager doubtless assured Ratcliffe that the arrangement was a bribe, and that in return you would pronounce a living man dead."

"There *was* something a bit shifty about the way he put it," said Babbage, reflecting. "I believe he may have actually winked, now I think of it." A shadow of dark surmise came over his face as he regarded Lager. "You mean to say that if this one had stayed the course I'd be free of this albatross?"

"Well, yes, but then you'd also be an accessory to murder, so, silver lining and all that," I said. "Lager has saved you the inscrutable moral dilemma of whether or not to pervert the course of justice for personal gain."

"No I didn't," insisted Lager.

"Yes, you did," I reminded him. "You congratulated your uncle Ratcliffe on a fine performance, relieved his pistol of its ramrod, and plunged it into his heart. Time being short, you then cleaned your weapon on Ratcliffe's shirtfront, leaving another tell-tale smudge, and dropped your weapon onto the floor, just as Victoria returned with Mister Babbage. Then, when you went to collect me, Victoria blurred the message with the toe of her shoe."

"Oh, very well," steamed Vicks. She stepped to the chafing dish with a sort resigned, up-jigging swagger, and helped herself to the decanter. "I don't suppose it matters now. I didn't want any evidence that Ratcliffe had survived Hadley."

"But then, before you could clean off the blood, Miss Belsize relieved you of the shoes to add to her collection…"

"Going to clean them, wasn't I?" claimed the maid.

"Most wise," I said. "Doubtless the discerning market for second-hand umbrellas and shoes has an acquired prejudice against blood stains. But before you could realise a profit, Mister Brickstock stumbled upon your cache of treasures when he went looking for his umbrella, and instead found the leverage he needed to force Miss Tenpenny to accept his proposal of marriage. Unfortunately for Mister Brickstock, Lager overheard the argument."

"I didn't hear anything, Anty," claimed Lager, with a weak, weary assertion, like the air slowly leaving an inflatable raft as it approaches a whirlpool.

"Of course you did, Lager old beanstalk," I said. "You claimed that you couldn't make out what was said, because you were in the garden, but when you spoke to me from the street when I found myself in the very same spot I heard you clearly. You should stay as close to the truth as possible, when fibbing, old man. You'll do well to remember that next time you carry out an elaborate plot to pilfer millions."

"Kimberly said that, as his wife, he'd be able to protect me from eventualities like the police finding out about the shoe," explained Vicks.

"Ham-handed and beneath contempt," I said. "And yet, appreciably more subtle than that for which I'd have given him credit. He wouldn't tell you where the shoes were, I take it."

"Just that they were safe."

"Then he grossly overestimated Chancy, in my view, but his reasoning was sound — he couldn't afford to let the shoes be found by you or anyone else, so he simply mailed them to himself, care of a firm of solicitors with which he had only the most remote of connections."

"Was this the insight Mister Brickstock had for me?" asked Ivor.

"It was not," I replied. "Mister Brickstock had his inspiration before finding the shoes and it was simply this — like me, he had observed that the shots were several seconds apart."

"Didn't you all say that you didn't hear the shots?" asked Ivor with reproach.

"You may take it that they were lying, Inspector," I said. "Two gunshots in a quiet cul-de-sac are not going to pass unnoticed and, take note, Miss Belsize heard them from the back of number three. Lager and Vicks both knew that the duel was going to take place, but only Lager knew that the contest had been fixed. They all also knew, of course, that duelling is illegal, and that's why Ratcliffe was going to play dead — to avoid being charged with murder."

"How utterly contemptible." Vicks cast this judgement at Lager over a full snifter.

"To be entirely fair, Miss Tenpenny," I said, "you weren't above queering the pitch yourself when you spotted the message on the floor. And you were going to marry Mister Brickstock rather than confess to it."

"It would have amounted to testifying that Ratcliffe had outlived my uncle."

"Well, just so, you couldn't have that," I agreed. "And neither could Lager. If Mister Brickstock were to reveal evidence that you had been the killer, then one could only conclude that the victim had been Hadley, and that he had therefore died second, and so he had to get the shoe back. He lured Mister Brickstock to Wedge Hedge Square with a note, doubtless with the intention of opening peaceful negotiations, but things got out of hand, didn't they Lager? And you stabbed Mister Brickstock right there, in the hall."

"How's that possible?" asked Vicks. "What about all the blood? The mess?"

"Lager cleaned it up," I explained. "He struggled with Kimberly Brickstock and, owing to the decided advantage of an enormous knife, got the better of him. Mister Brickstock escaped, though, and barricaded himself in the reading room where, sadly, he expired."

"But we were all together at number one when it happened," complained Vicks.

"No, we weren't," I gently corrected. "I don't know where you were, but when Mister Brickstock was murdered I was at an evening performance of *Hold Everything* at the Palladium."

"That's ridiculous."

"I know," I sympathised. "The story was all right but the choreography was all over the shop. Still, there was the full-sized boxing ring in the final act and some snappy numbers — I haven't been able to get '*You're The Cream In My Coffee*' out of my head for days."

"No, I mean, we heard the service bell," pointed out Vicks. "And didn't you say that a taxi brought Burly here yesterday morning?"

"A taxi brought Lager here yesterday morning, from Claridge's, where he'd reserved a table and enjoyed breakfast under the name of Kimberly Brickstock. He even had a message sent to himself, inviting him here."

"I say, Anty," Chancy spoke up, now. He'd been wandering the room for a bit, teasing the candles, but was in the moment struck by a concern. "I think you're overlooking something. You said the note was found in

Mister Brickstock's pocket. How could Lager have got the note into his pocket, if you follow my reasoning, if he only received it the morning after?"

"The note said the same thing, Chancy old melon, but it wasn't the same note," I explained.

"This was the point of requiring Chard the sarcastic page boy to read it aloud. Lager was counting on the famously acute observational skills of the five-star page boy, but he underestimated those of Chard, who recalled that his variation on the Brickstock theme left without finishing his breakfast."

"He's never walked away from a crumb in his life," said Vicks.

"Indeed not," I said, sadly. "And he never will."

"Well, I'm convinced." Vicks lowered a Beak Street glower on the accused. Then she turned a King's Council quizzical eye on me. "Hang on — who rang the service bell then?"

"Lucifer did that," I said. "As evidenced by the birth and baptismal certificates."

"I think you're going to have to explain that, too," suggested Quip, with a proprietary attitude toward the subject.

"Not the certificates themselves," I accommodated, "but the manner of their arrival."

"I sent them by post," said Quip, with an implied 'what else, homing pigeon?'

"And they arrived — in the letterbox."

"Where should they have wound up?"

"Oh, the garden. Or the gate-hedge," I recalled. "Anywhere but the letterbox, particularly if the postman heard Lucifer's mid-season terrace chant, which he could hardly have failed to do. The postman, however, is a sportsman, and typically gets as close as he can to actually making a delivery. Yesterday, at eleven-thirty, he could hear the enemy but he could not see him, because Lager had lured Lucifer away with two pounds of chopped lamb that he had appropriated from the kitchen of number three. He brought the dog to the service entrance of number one and tied him to a cord that led to the bell-panel. We know that any bell-pull in any of the three houses operates on the bell-panel in all three service halls, and obviously the opposite is true as well."

Lager, too, had been pacing the room for a bit in a deliberately nomadic motif that happened to bring him to the door. Constable Constable drew himself up within his rug and, in that way that only a bobby can, put on his bobby's helmet. Lager turned sheepishly back to the room.

"I'd list the key areas where you went wrong, Lager," I said. "But frankly they're legion. I've forgotten half of them already. You showed poor form out of the gate, however, when you assumed that the old club tie was enough for me to back up your claim to the Tenpenny Tontine. It's not, and it never could be…" I caught Quip's eye and I fancy she was bathing me in that gaze that girls pack in spares when they go to see Valentino pictures. "…my reputation for unsticking the wicket on behalf of friends and family has always hinged on one vital point — said friends and family haven't killed anyone."

Lager made a couple of false starts on pleas that sounded something like 'hamina-ma-hamina' and 'wuh-huh-blimey' before settling on a coherent line of defence.

"It's nowhere near as bad as you make out, Anty. It was all Uncle Ratcliffe's idea, don't you know. Wanted me to have the pot, while I was still young, what?"

"I might have let you offer that defence to the court, Lager," I countered. "Even though I know it's bosh of the purest grain, had you not crossed the line and tried to eliminate a not only innocent but, I daresay, heroically dutiful Scottish Terrier. That's before even accounting for the loss of the inspector's notebook to which, I can tell you, he was very much attached. So, sorry, no outs. You murdered your uncle and I can — and I will — prove it."

Lager addressed the larger court of public opinion now, which he seemed to feel was best represented by Quip, doubtless on the grounds that she knew him least.

"You can't believe that Uncle Ratcliffe thought he could get away with pretending to be dead indefinitely."

"Of course he did." I also addressed Quip, for reasons which will become clear momentarily. "He was going to simply disappear, and he could have done it, too, because Ratcliffe Tenpenny never existed."

This was met, understandably, with a communal expression of general amazement which I herein characterise as a single, "Eh?"

"Once declared dead, Ratcliffe Tenpenny was going to return to Plug's Gutter and his old identity...." I once again addressed Quip. "...your father."

# CHAPTER NINETEEN

# The Twist in the Tale of the Tenpenny Tontine

It was Ivor who drew the curtain on our cliffhanger with the pretext that he already had all the guilty parties he required for his purposes, plus a full trouser's worth of cellar water. He and Constable Pen Constable took Lager away into the night and the rest of us agreed to meet at Chancy's office the following day for tea and twists.

I had felt, what with the storm and damp and rising above the guinea stamp of rank to bring a Juniper to justice, entitled to an extended drift among the down-filled, and it was fully noon before I was clipping down Lombard Street beneath a serene and settled cyan sky that appeared to have worked out all its issues the night before.

Chancy's offices, as earlier divulged, were above a rollicking tea shop, and its winds wafted with the perfume of the East. The effect persisted into the cabinet room where Chancy had laid on two silver tea services, coffee, and an ingenious replica of the dome of Saint Paul's composed of digestive biscuits — chocolate topped, too, and not the repellant plain ones.

"What ho, inquisitive minds," I called as I approached the desk on which this lavish effort to impress had been staged. Gathered about the display, distributed on chairs and boxes and foot were, in order of irritability, Babbage by a furlong, Miss Belsize in very nearly a dead heat with Vicks, Quip, well in their dust, and Chancy, smiling at the starting gate.

"You took your country vicar's time," observed Vicks.

"I was unavoidably detained," I explained. "I had to stop in at the Juniper for a bite — my man made *crêpes aux framboises avec coulé de shoe polish* for breakfast. Also, I felt I had to let the games committee know that Lager wouldn't be fulfilling his role as hawker at tonight's charity auction of unclaimed toppers, capes, and copies of *Lady Chatterley's Lover.*"

Chancy perked up at something in this. "Oh, I say, Anty, at the risk of appearing to jockey misfortune, any chance you could put me up for membership, now there's an opening?"

"I'm afraid not, Chancy old brief," I said. "I was told just this morning that you remain wholly and enduringly blackballed."

"Oh, right. Well, thanks for asking, in any case."

"I didn't, actually," I recollected. "It was mentioned preemptively."

"Can we get to the business at hand?" asked Vicks.

"Absolutely," I agreed. "Coffee, I think, just as it comes, and one of those cinnamon spires."

Chancy played mother and Vicks played *The March of the British Grenadiers* on the desk with her fingertips.

"You gave us to understand that you had some insight

into the disposition of the tontine," said Vicks in admirably measured tones.

"And I do," I said, walking my coffee and biscuit to the window so they could have a good look at the giant teacup.

"And what's all this about my father and Hadley Tenpenny?" asked Quip. "My father is Wist Keats."

"I know," I said. "I'm afraid I have some bad news for you. On reflection, I might have presented this better."

"Well, you've plenty of time to start over, Anty," said Quip. "Because I have no idea what you're on about."

"Your father was presented to Terrence Tenpenny as the illegitimate issue of his affair with Hespenal Halisham-Lewes. His likeness and letters were almost certainly also sent to Sir Bromley Baker, and Tobias Lord Trilby, and Casey Cooley, Bishop of Scilly, at the very least, all of whom also had relationships with the energetic Miss Halisham-Lewes."

"In aid of what?" asked Quip.

"The ancient art of fleecing the common or garden mark," I answered. "All of these men were given to believe that they had fathered sons and, owing to what I like to think of as a double-entendre — their rank in society — they could not acknowledge them, but instead hid their saplings of shame in the forest of orphans that is Gutter Folly, under the care of Willow Willoughby."

"The vaccination certificate," surmised Quip.

"Exactly. No child born after 1853 would have been allowed into school without one, and I think that if you examine the parish records you'll find any number of boys about your father's age who nevertheless got by without such a thing — Wist Keats could only be vaccinated so often, but with the happy cooperation of the worldly

Reverend Davidy Lloyd, he could be reborn as many times as there were paying customers."

"You're saying my father and this bloke Ratcliffe Tenpenny, whom I've never met, are the same person."

"I am," I said. "What's more I can prove it. You're familiar with your grandmother's writing desk? The one with the infinite supply of stationery?"

"Of course."

"Can you describe it?"

"I suppose," Quip looked about her, as one does at school when called upon to recite. "It's a writing desk, as you say. Rickety old thing. There's an ink pot, pigeon holes, photographs…"

"…pictures of your father as a child."

"Yes, well, she lives in the past a bit, does my nan."

"The point is that they're the same pictures which Ratcliffe Tenpenny kept on his mantlepiece — pictures of himself in happier times."

"This makes no sense," objected Vicks. "How could Ratcliffe possibly have been living a double-life?"

"I think that Quip can answer that as well as I can," I suggested.

"He was always in prison," she said. "Or so we thought. He'd come home for a month, every once in a while, and then be off again on some adventure."

"And the few who might miss him at Wedge Hedge Square believed him to be in spiritual retreat at a Carthusian monastery," I completed the picture.

"But, why?"

"Because he was an immoral reprobate, Quip, with a set of core values at which an alley cat would shake his head in despair," I said, choosing my words carefully. "Sorry."

"No, you're right. He was."

"Doubtless he planned an honourable career in the acquisition and transportation of fine wines and spirits, but when Terrence Tenpenny activated the spare he took on the dual role of absent father and sole heir." I paused to sip dramatically of my coffee, and nibble meaningfully of my biscuit. "This was in his twenty-first year — just about when Wist Keats came into his little all and sailed for France where, according to his diaphanous cover story, he remained as a guest of the state for several months."

"I have to admit it, Anty," said Vicks with a festive intonation that sounded decidedly forced, like when people sing along when they know the words but not the tune. "May I call you Anty? I have to admit it, I didn't think much of you at first glance but Lager, for his countless faults, was right about you — you really have sorted it all out."

"Modesty forbids."

"What a tremendous relief this is." Vicks melted into her chair. "You have anything stronger than this, Chancy old thing? I feel like celebrating."

"What's the occasion?" I asked.

Vicks laughed along with what she took to be the joke. "The tontine, of course. It doesn't matter anymore who died first or second — Ratcliffe was never a Tenpenny."

"Yes, he was."

"He was never. You just said so."

"No, I said that he never existed. Wist Keats, however, did, and he, too, was a Tenpenny."

"He was a Keats," insisted Vicks. "Let him lay claim to the Keats tontine, if there is one."

"Like everyone in Gutter Folly with a paternity selected from the pantheon of Romantic poets, Wist Keats was an illegitimate child," I explained. "But his father did recognise him, distantly, when he left a legacy for all remaining members of the Tontine Generation — Ratcliffe, Hadley, and Wist."

"You mean... my nan, and Terrence Tenpenny..." Quip appeared, briefly, scandalised, and then considered the point more closely, "Actually, no, that sounds about right."

"That doesn't prove a thing," declared Vicks.

"It doesn't need to," I said. "Because Wist Keats was, legally, Ratcliffe Coleridge, and in his twenty-first year his father formally recognised him. The tontine belongs to his nearest heir, which would that be, Chancy? His mother, Willow Willoughby or his daughter, Quip?"

Chancy blinked at me over a placid cup of tea.

"No idea, Anty," he said. "Frankly, I'm a little lost. I abandoned the trail somewhere in Belgium, I think."

"France, I think you'll find," I said. "No matter, Chancy, if you'll just give an opinion on the following — what happens to the tontine if there's some dispute over the legal claim of the beneficiaries?"

"Ah." Chancy crossed his legs and balanced his saucer on his knee in a most professorial manner. "That would be decided by the Chancery Division of the High Court."

"And what would be their likely determination?"

"They'd award the lot to the crown."

"They'd award the lot to the crown," I repeated for Vicks' sake. "So there you have it. Either Wist Keats died a Tenpenny and died second, or the state just goes out and buys another bridge or colony or whatever takes its fancy."

Vicks gave Quip a guarded, sideline squint, and Quip smiled sweetly back.

"What are you proposing, Boisjoly?" asked Vicks.

"Lager's original plan."

"Lager's plan," echoed Vicks. "The one that left three people dead and got him arrested? That plan?"

"No sense letting it go to waste. With a simple variation it might be salvaged."

"What variation is that?"

"Equity," I said. "Quip will inherit the tontine. She has no need nor, I'm baffled to say, appreciation for London, so she will apportion to you Wedge Hedge Square and a substantial development fund, so that you might buy Mister Babbage's property."

"I vote for Mister Boisjoly's plan," declared Babbage.

"In turn, Mister Babbage will do exactly what he planned to do anyway, which is nothing at all," I continued. "Miss Belsize, too, will receive a generous pension and one of the houses that you'll build in the to-be-named new development — I mention, apropos of nothing at all, that to date there is no Boisjoly Gardens in the city of London. There's a Boisjoly Mews on the Isle of Dogs, but it's an ironic name for a sluice gate."

"I could fix up Drab House." As she'd done the last time she was in Chancy's office, Quip gazed longingly toward Gutter Folly, but this time with shimmering hope welling up in her eyes.

A beautiful woman with tears in her eyes operates on the hard Boisjoly heart in much the same way a blast furnace operates on a tallow-wax candle. But of course, it was never meant to be — Quip Keats couldn't bear London and I couldn't bear anywhere else for long.

"You'll need assistance... expertise..." I said. "The place is a death trap and it's sinking into the swamp. I recommend that you immediately take on an architectural engineer. If you can find one that can recite *Praktikê* with any proficiency, so much the better."

"Oh, I say..." Chancy put down his cup and waved his hand. "...I can recite *Praktikê.*"

"And you're an architectural engineer with no career prospects in London, now that your last major trust has been dissolved."

"Oh, right. That's true, isn't it."

"Say you'll do it, Chancy," implored Quip. "Come to Gutter Folly and help me dig the north-east tower out of the swamp."

"You're a wealthy woman," I said. "You could fill in the irrigation canal and return Gutter Folly to the former glory of Drab-on-Drabble."

"Could I?"

"Of course," assured Chancy with a heretofore unexpressed authority. "And then you could drain the swamps."

"That will take time, though," I pointed out. "And in the interim, you'll need some system or mechanism to prevent the residents of Drab House Retirement Home for Rogues from wandering into sinkholes — you'll hardly have time for that sort of surveillance in future. What you need is a conscientious Scottish Terrier with a lively sense of transport links and a yearning for purpose."

❧

234

The spring air still had that *après le déluge* crisp clarity that manages to make even the horses smell freshly laundered. The sun was angled over Lombard Street as though hung there by the lighting director of the Palladium, casting the complex creases and corners of the eclectic stone façades into high relief, and the swaying signage as swinging silhouettes on the pavement.

I clipped up the sidewalk in the very rough direction of Kensington, tapping my umbrella on the pavement in time to something I was whistling in my head, when Babbage caught up to me. He grasped my arm and used it to keep pace a-starboard side.

"This is a most satisfactory conclusion to the affair, Mister Boisjoly," he positively sang. "Most satisfactory indeed."

"Glad you like it, Mister Babbage," I said. "I picked it out specially for you."

"Nothing wrong in it, either, is there?" he said, in a distinctly rhetorical tone. "Guilty party's been caught. We know how it was done, thanks to you — no value in any sort of inquest. Dashed waste of time and resources."

"Absolutely, Mister Babbage," I assured him. "You may do the bare minimum required by law in good conscience."

"Just so, just so." From the corner of my eye I could see that Babbage was rubbing his hands together in warm anticipation of a lazy afternoon.

We walked on for a bit in silence, breathing in the good spring air and, in my case, thinking of nothing at all. Babbage, however, was reminiscing.

"Couldn't do the same in your father's case, of course."

Babbage stated this as though it was obviously something that we were both thinking.

Indeed, the point wasn't very far from my thoughts and hadn't been since Vickers came back into my employ, some months ago, and made the connection between a hired assassin of our mutual acquaintance and the young lady my mother had engaged to be my father's private secretary, just a week or so before he tripped into the path of an electric tram in Shepherd's Bush. Had I the dizzy credulity of a newborn Chancy Proctor, I might have ascribed the connection to Vickers' patchwork recall, but as it was I felt that one day in the future, possibly quite soon, there would be a reckoning.

"Of course, Mister Babbage" I agreed, with the tone of idle banter. "Tell me something, did Mama express an interest in whether or not there was an inquest?

"Your mother?" asked Babbage. "Oh, yes. She was very clear about it — she didn't want the family put through the embarrassment of a public inquiry into your father's passing."

"Too late by then, though, I take it," I surmised.

"Hmm? No, not at all," said Babbage. "She stated her position preemptively — about a week before he died, in fact. Rather a coincidence, now I think of it."

# Anty Boisjoly Mysteries

I hope you enjoyed *The Tale of the Tenpenny Tontine.* I know I did, even though and probably especially because it's the most involved Anty Boisjoly plot so far. That's not to say that the others are essentially a retelling of Jack & Jill, so if you haven't read them yet I offer the below for your consideration…

## The Case of the Canterfell Codicil
*The First Anty Boisjoly Mystery*
In *The Case of the Canterfell Codicil,* Wodehousian gadabout and clubman Anty Boisjoly takes on his first case when his old Oxford chum and coxswain is facing the gallows, accused of the murder of his wealthy uncle. Not one but two locked-room mysteries later, Boisjoly's pitting his wits and witticisms against a subversive butler, a senile footman, a single-minded detective-inspector, an irascible goat, and the eccentric conventions of the pastoral Sussex countryside to untangle a multi-layered mystery of secret bequests, ancient writs, love triangles, revenge, and a teasing twist in the final paragraph.

## The Case of the Ghost of Christmas Morning
*The Christmas number*
In *The Case of the Ghost of Christmas Morning,* clubman, *flaneur,* idler and sleuth Anty Boisjoly pits his sardonic wits against another pair of impossible murders. This time, Anty Boisjoly's Aunty Boisjoly is the only possible suspect when a murder victim stands his old friends a farewell drink at the local, hours after being murdered.

## The Tale of the Tenpenny Tontine
*The one you just read*
It's another mystifying, manor house murder for bon-vivant and problem-solver Anty Boisjoly, when his clubmate asks him to determine who died first after a duel is fought in a locked room. The untold riches of the Tenpenny Tontine are in the balance, but the stakes only get higher when Anty determines that, duel or not, this was a case of murder.

## The Case of the Carnaby Castle Curse
*The scary one*
The ancient curse of Carnaby Castle has begun taking victims again — either that, or someone's very cleverly done away with the new young bride of the philandering family patriarch, and the chief suspect is none other than Carnaby, London's finest club steward.

Anty Boisjoly's wits and witticisms are tested to their frozen limit as he sifts the superstitions, suspicions, and age-old schisms of the mediaeval Peak District village of Hoy to sort out how it was done before the curse can claim Carnaby himself.

## Reckoning at the Riviera Royale
*The one with Anty's mum (due in 2022)*
Anty finally has that awkward 'did you murder my father' conversation with his mother while finding himself in the ticklish position of defending her and an innocent elephant against charges of impossible murder.